"Did you know," he said, "that by candlelight, your hair shines with traces of a most remarkable burnished red?"

"You mean like dead leaves," she said hoarsely.

"No, I mean like flames," he murmured. Burrowing beneath her hair, his hand covered the nape of her neck. Gently, but inexorably, he pulled her forward.

As his face drew near, Audra closed her eyes, bracing herself. But his lips merely brushed across hers in a feather-light whisper. The contact was so light, so fleeting, it tantalized her somehow. Almost involuntarily, she uttered a soft protest when he drew back.

His mouth descended upon hers again, this time hard enough to make her aware of his heat, ruthless enough to set the whole room to spinning.

Also by Susan Carroll
Published by Fawcett Books:

THE LADY WHO HATED SHAKESPEARE
THE SUGAR ROSE
BRIGHTON ROAD
THE BISHOP'S DAUGHTER

THE
WOOING
OF
MISS
MASTERS

Susan Carroll

FAWCETT CREST • NEW YORK

A Fawcett Crest Book
Published by Ballantine Books
Copyright © 1991 by Susan Coppula

All rights reserved under International and Pan-American Copyright Conventions. Published in the United States by Ballantine Books, a division of Random House, Inc., New York, and simultaneously in Canada by Random House of Canada Limited, Toronto.

Library of Congress Catalog Card Number: 91-92112

ISBN 0-449-21952-6

Printed in Canada

First Edition: November 1991

To my uncle Sam and to Mark Petersen, the gentleman who helps me take care of him.

CHAPTER 1

The Duke of Raeburn was in a black humor.

The signs had been noted by His Grace's household throughout the castle that morning, as carefully as sailors reading the sky, then battening down the hatches for the approaching storm. Most of the staff strove to stay out of the duke's way, from the laundry maid to the stately butler, all of them walking about on tiptoe.

The only one who remained unaffected was John Farley, the head groom. But then he had been employed at Castle Raeburn some fifty years. He had known the present duke since the days when he had been but Lord Simon. Consequently, while the rest of the servants skittered about doing their tasks, Farley lingered near the suit of armor mounted in the front hall while he chewed meditatively on a wisp of straw.

His cap doffed, there was no disrespect in his mien but no fear either as he watched the duke come stalking through the archway at the far end of the vast chamber.

Early morning light filtered through narrow windows, which were sealed with heavy leaded glass. The gloom-ridden hall was the only surviving part of the medieval section of the castle with its barrel-vaulted roof and stark stone walls displaying a formidable array of swords, halberds, and battle-axes. Farley thought most modern gentlemen in their yellow breeches and frilled cravats looked rather foolish in such a setting.

But not so His Grace.

The duke was a large man with massive shoulders, built like a block of granite. As he strode into the hall, one half expected to see a squire come rushing forward to tug gauntlets upon those powerful hands, to toss a coat of chain mail over that broad chest.

Despite the fashionable cut of his dark blue riding coat, His Grace conveyed the impression of one who had stepped from another century when men were bred of iron. His hair swept back from his brow and shagged against his starched collar, the unrelenting blackness of those thick locks broken only by flecks of silver at his temples. He had inherited the Raeburn hawklike nose and square jaw, but the heavy forbidding brows and the eyes of blue-tempered steel were all His Grace's own.

His face had tanned so deep as to almost give him a foreign appearance like some Barbary Coast sea captain, deep crags set at either side of his mouth. Most said those weather-beaten lines were the result of His Grace having traveled so much in heathen climates, but Farley allowed as it was because the duke rarely ever smiled.

The groom had heard tell once how some fancy gentlemen in London had proposed a wager as to when if ever His Grace might be likely to grin. But nothing had come of it as no one had dared write Raeburn's name in the betting books, the duke's temper being as legendary as his famous frown.

Farley noted that that ominous scowl was more pronounced than ever as His Grace's top boots rang out upon the hall's rough stone floor. He tapped a riding crop against the leg of his buckskin breeches, the look of barely restrained anger upon his face enough to put most men into a quake. Therefore it was not surprising that the pretty young lady who trailed in the duke's wake appeared highly discomfited.

Looping the train of her riding habit over her arm, she fairly ran to catch up with His Grace while essaying a laugh, which Farley supposed was meant to be a flirtatious giggle, but came out more as a nervous titter.

"I never meant to be such a trouble to Your Grace. Goodness me! I simply don't know how I came to be lost upon your estate or have my horse pull a shoe."

"Nor I, either, madam," came the cold reply. "But I shall have my carriage brought round to see you home."

"Oh, n-no, pray, you must not go to such bother. I do not mind in the least waiting until my horse has been reshod." She gave the duke a look that would have melted a heart of stone, but Farley reckoned that the young lady had never come up against a man entirely made of granite before.

"Believe me, it is no bother at all to send you upon your way, Miss Long." The duke seemed to produce the housekeeper out of thin air with a gesture of the riding crop, but in truth, Mrs. Bede had been hovering anxiously in the background the entire time.

"Your Grace?" The housekeeper ducked into a hasty curtsy.

"See to Miss Long's comfort until the carriage is brought round."

Miss Long started to emit a faint cry of protest but His Grace favored her with one of his dagger-like stares while running the length of the crop suggestively between his fingers.

The lady stared at the crop, swallowed, and said no more.

"Your servant, madam." The duke made a stiff bow as the housekeeper led the girl away. It was difficult to tell whether the expression upon Miss Long's lovely face reflected more of disappointment or relief.

As the two women vanished beneath the arch, the duke's gaze turned toward Farley. When His Grace beckoned, Farley snapped to attention.

"What progress have the stables made with that young woman's horse?"

"The mare will be reshod in no time, Your Grace." Farley scratched one of his few remaining tufts of hair. "It's a curious thing, Your Grace, but that horse appears to have been outfitted recently with a new set of shoes. How one could have worked loose so soon—"

"I am sure you know as well as I how that horse came to be missing a shoe, John. What I want to know is whether the mare is fit to be led back to Miss Long's home?"

"Yes, Your Grace."

"Then dispatch one of the stable boys to do so at once and have Parker hurry along with that carriage."

"Yes, Your Grace."

Farley whipped about smartly to execute these

orders. But he had not taken two steps when he was halted by the sound of the duke's voice.

"And John ..."

Farley glanced back.

"If any more young ladies lose their way in my woods—"

"Yes, Your Grace?"

"Throw them into the moat."

"Very good, Your Grace." Farley gave a respectful touch to the side of his cap. Not until he was well outside the castle walls did he permit himself to break into a broad grin.

"I don't see anything amusing about the entire incident." Simon Arthur Lakeland, the sixth Duke of Raeburn, was still growling long after the intrusive Miss Long had been transported from his castle. Ensconced behind the glossy surface of a mahogany writing desk in his library, he glared at his companion who made no effort to disguise her mirth.

The library afforded an excellent selection of comfortable divans and settees, but Lady Augusta Penrose had drawn up a quaint maid of honor chair, well suited to her petite frame. A dark-haired woman, her elegant clothes spoke of town bronze, her twinkling eyes of unfailing good humor.

Lady Augusta was one of the few who dared to laugh at Raeburn. But then Augusta never could be brought to show a proper respect for her older brother, even if she was just a bit of a thing, scarce coming up to his shoulder. She had the Raeburn nose, but not the family height.

When the duke had complained to his sister about his unexpected visitor, Lady Augusta had immediately gone off into whoops from which she had yet to recover.

"Oh the p-poor girl," she managed to gasp out. "Imagine all the t-trouble she went to, discovering your habit of riding out early, removing her horse's shoe, setting up the scene for a romantic rescue, awaiting her fair knight. And instead she gets you, l-looking like the very devil, I daresay."

"It was a vulgar ploy merely to make my acquaintance—even worse than that chit in the inn yard yesterday."

"Oh? You didn't tell me about her."

"Some yellow-haired wench I'd never set eyes on before. She feigned a swoon in front of me."

"What!" Lady Augusta's eyes danced. "Right into your arms?"

"Not in my arms." Raeburn said with grim satisfaction. "I let her plop onto her bottom into the mud. *That* I assure you, roused her fast enough."

This sent Augusta off into fresh peals of laughter until tears stood in her eyes. "Oh, Simon, you are so dreadfully unchivalrous."

"I can be chivalrous enough to a *lady*, but these baggages! What is amiss with these modern hurly-burly females? Don't any of them possess delicacy of mind or regard for proper conduct?"

Lady Augusta dabbed her handkerchief at her moist eyes. "Oh, dear. You are beginning to sound more like Papa every day."

Since their late, esteemed parent had been both high in the instep and full of starch, Simon did not take this to be a compliment.

"Besides," Augusta added. "All these vexing incidents with the ladies throwing themselves at your head are entirely your own fault."

"My fault?" Simon said thunderstruck. He straightened so abruptly, the leather of his chair creaked in protest.

"Yes, my dear." Smiling, she quoted, " 'It is a truth universally acknowledged, that a single man in possession of a good fortune must be in want of a wife.' "

Simon winced. He had enjoyed the wry humor to be found in *Pride and Prejudice* as much as his sister, but the gentle gibe contained in the novel's opening sentence did not seem near so amusing when applied to himself.

"Blast it all," he said. "Looking for a wife is exactly what I've been doing, this past month and more." He was fully conscious of the fact he would turn thirty-seven before the year was out, and the nursery upstairs yet remained empty. Although Simon did not always do his duty with the best of grace, at least, by God, he did it.

"It's only that I never expected to be regarded as some sort of a prize," he continued to complain. "Sometimes I think we might just as well set up a greased pole competition, only award me instead of the pig."

Augusta threw up one hand imploringly. "Please, Simon. You have made my sides ache enough already."

"It is all very well for you to laugh. I think you are more to blame for the antics of these blasted women than anyone. That confounded notion of yours that I should give a ball! You've got 'em all stirred up."

"Why, you ungrateful wretch!" Augusta ex-

7

claimed. "And after I have been wearing myself nigh to the bone planning the affair for you. Remember it was you who commanded me to find some way of introducing you to all the eligible ladies in the county. What better way than inviting them all to a ball at Castle Raeburn? It seemed such a romantic notion, rather like that prince in the faery story."

"Rather like you are bent on making a damned cake of me," Simon groused.

Lady Augusta sniffed. "Well, if you feel that way about it, I am sure I don't know why I should go to such bother. Stanton was loath to let me come to you for so long anyway. I am sure he will be quite glad to have me home again." She arose briskly shaking out her skirts. "You may just hie yourself to London next Season with all the other bachelors and visit the Marriage Mart."

"Almack's? Good God! You know I look ridiculous in knee breeches. Besides I cannot abide London."

Augusta merely lifted her shoulders in an expressive shrug. When she really did appear on the verge of leaving, Simon bolted out of his chair, positioning himself in front of the door. He had never been any good at coaxing, but he gave her the half grimace that passed for his smile and said, "Don't fly up into the boughs, Gus. You know how I get when something happens to disrupt my early morning ride."

"Surly as a distempered bear," she agreed affably.

"That ride is my one solitary pleasure before I am set upon by bailiffs, land agents, and complaining tenants. I didn't appreciate being plagued be-

8

fore breakfast by some scheming female, but I don't mean to snap at you. You must know how grateful I am for everything you've been trying to do for me. It's just this whole business of being in the market for a bride." He expelled his breath in a heavy sigh. "Well, it's not exactly like going to the horse auction and picking out a good hunter, is it?"

As much as she struggled to repress it, Augusta's dimpled smile peeked out again. "Poor Simon," she mocked, but her eyes warmed with sympathy.

"Why can't you just pick out some chit for me?" he appealed to her, only half jesting. "Some sensible young woman who would know how to conduct herself, one who wouldn't chatter too much. She wouldn't even have to be a beauty as long as she doesn't have a face like a monkey. God knows I don't have many requirements."

"No, you don't," she agreed sadly.

"Would you like me to have more?"

"I would like you to fall in love."

Simon pinched her chin. "Stanton's been reading you too much of that romantic poetry again."

But this time Augusta didn't smile. She said rather thickly, "I had always hoped, Simon, that you would find the happiness in marriage that I have found."

"Ah, but yours is a match made in heaven, my dear. Extremely rare. I never looked for such a thing, I promise you. I never expected to have to marry at all." His mood darkened again. "Any more than I ever expected to awake one morning and find myself the Duke of Raeburn."

Abruptly he turned away from her and strode to the window to stare out. Set between the bookcases, the tall, mullioned panels of glass overlooked the vista at the rear of the house. Castle Raeburn was one of the few manors in Sussex, perhaps all of England, to be still surrounded by a moat. Just below Simon, swans sailed by in regal splendor, barely seeming to raise a ripple in the cloudy waters. In the distance loomed the shadowy outline of the deer park and woodland—oaks, larches, and elms stretching as far as the eye could see.

The lord of all he surveyed, Simon thought with a bitter sneer. Except that he had never felt himself to be anything other than a usurper, filling a pair of shoes cut to someone else's size.

Lost in this gloomy contemplation, he wasn't aware of Augusta slipping up beside him until she spoke softly, "Even after all this time, it's never gotten any easier for you, has it, Simon?"

His only reply was a curt shake of his head. But then Augusta knew better than anyone how little he had ever coveted the title, or these lands, how much he loathed his inheritance, especially the way it had come to him.

Almost as one, the two of them turned involuntarily to stare at the portrait mounted over the fireplace. Encased within an ornate gilt frame was the painting of a man with dark curls, the infamous Raeburn nose set between laughing blue eyes. He sat perched upon a wooden stile, a hunting dog at his feet, a riding crop held carelessly in his grasp. The artist had captured all of Robert Lakeland's impatience with posing so well, Simon frequently expected his brother to leap out of the frame and go tearing off in search of more exciting pursuits.

Except, of course, that the late Duke of Raeburn would never do so again.

Simon averted his gaze, feeling the familiar ache of loss, little dulled by seven years passage of time. He felt Augusta slip her arm comfortingly through his.

"I was still in the schoolroom when Robert died," she mused. "He was so much older than me I never felt as if I got to know him very well. What was he like?"

"Oh, top of the trees," Simon said gruffly, unable even for Augusta to find the words to convey what Robert had meant to him. He still carried with him much of the younger brother's awe for the older sibling who had taught him to ride, to shoot, to drive to an inch. When Simon had received his first black eye at Eton, it had been Robert who had descended upon the school in a blaze of magnificence to teach Simon to be so handy with his fives, he had never been milled down again.

It had been Robert who had come to sit up with him all night when their father and mother had died of a fever within days of each other. The two brothers had shared a bottle of port even as they had shared their grief in a silence that needed no words. And it had been Robert who had proudly buckled the sword to his little brother's side when Simon had received his first commission as a cavalry officer.

But these memories of Robert faded as they always did in the face of that final grim one. Simon supposed he ought to be grateful at least that he had been home on leave from the army that cold winter's day, or else he would never have been there at the castle, never been able to bid his brother ... farewell.

Simon had always told Robert he would be

brought home on a hurdle someday, all because of that neck-or-nothing way in which he rode. It had been a jest between the two of them, nothing more, the younger brother presuming to chafe his elder.

But all laughter seemed to have stilled forever that morning when Robert was borne back from the hunting field upon a litter. His neck had not been broken; that perhaps would have been a mercy compared to the agonizing hours that followed.

His ribs crushed, bleeding inwardly, Robert had descended painfully into the arms of death, and there had been naught Simon could do for him but remain at his side, bringing what comfort he could. Simon had never been given to displays of emotion, but he had allowed the tears to course down his cheeks, unashamed, making no effort to check them.

Despite his agony, Robert had possessed enough strength to touch Simon's hand while summoning up that familiar lopsided smile.

"It'll be all right, Simon. Truly it will," he had whispered. "You'll make a far better duke than me. . . ."

But then, hadn't that been just like Robert? *He* had been the one who lay dying, and yet he had struggled to reassure Simon. The memory of those final moments with his brother still had the power to bring a burning ache into Simon's throat.

He coughed to clear it. Realizing that Augusta regarded him with anxious eyes, he sought to change the subject. He tried to make his voice light. "Yes, Robert was a splendid fellow, though it was damned inconsiderate of him not to have left a son behind to save my neck from the matrimonial noose."

"But he left two charming daughters," Augusta reminded him.

"True. How do Maria and the girls get on in their new home?"

"Quite wonderfully. Maria enjoys being nearer to town."

Simon was glad to hear that. After his brother's death, he had entreated his sister-in-law and nieces to consider the castle still their home, but Maria had gently refused. Simon knew she had been wise to do so. It had been painful for her seeing another take her husband's place, as painful as it had been for Simon to assume that role. After living for some years in the Dower House, Maria had recently moved to Kensington.

"Both the girls have grown so," Augusta enthused. "Do you realize that Elizabeth will be ready to make her come-out next Season? I wish Maria would let me present her. It will be ages before my own Emily is old enough for her first Season."

"It confounds me how you could be looking forward to such a thing, Gus. You positively enjoy making the rounds of all those infernal balls, hostessing crushing parties, helping insipid young misses and gawky youths find partners. I believe you were born to be one of those dreadful matchmaking mamas."

"I suppose I was," Lady Augusta said cheerfully, in no way troubled by the charge. "That is why I leaped at your invitation when you wrote to ask my help." But her face clouded over as she added, "However I shan't enjoy it in the least if I think the prospect of finding a bride makes you so utterly miserable. If you are not feeling quite ready, the ball could still be canceled, Simon."

Her words presented to him an awful temptation. Indeed he did wish the ball could be set aside, that he could simply close up the castle again and resume his travels on the Continent. But he had been running away for too many years.

"What! And disappoint all those ladies who seem to regard me as the catch of the Season?" Raeburn raised his brows, his voice laced with self-mockery. "After all, I am the sixth Duke of Raeburn. And we all know, a duke must have his duchess."

He stretched his arms, flexing his back muscles. "But enough talk of balls and weddings for one morning. Why don't you fling on your shawl and take a walk with me out to the paddock? I acquired a new bull at the market yesterday. A most capital fellow. He promises to do much for raising the stock of my cattle. If the heifers prove only half so eager as the young ladies hereabouts—"

But Augusta clapped her hands over her ears, greatly scandalized. She refused his invitation, saying that far too many details for the ball yet required her attention. "So you may cease your lewd comments and go view your horrid bull by yourself."

Simon nearly smiled. For all her acquired sophistication, Gus was still an adorable little prude. He was halfway out the study door when he turned and belatedly asked if there was anything he could do to help with the preparations.

She must have detected the reluctance with which he made the offer, for she grinned. "No, nothing, except to stay out of the way. Though you might practice being a little more gracious with the ladies. Your manners have gotten a trifle rusty."

"I never had any. It was always Robert who possessed the most address with your fair sex. I fear that I frighten most of the poor dears to death."

"And take great pleasure in doing so," Augusta said severely. "You can be perfectly charming when you wish. You might begin by being more gallant to the next lady who loses her way in your woods."

"Not on your life! I can tolerate being hunted, but I'll be damned if I'll be pursued when I've gone to earth on my own coverts." As he strode through the door, he added darkly, "God help the wench who ambushes me on my own lands again."

CHAPTER 2

The ball to be given at Castle Raeburn had formed the chief topic of drawing room conversation for the past sennight. It was inevitable that the subject would be discussed at Meadow Lane Lodge even though the lodge's current tenant, Miss Audra Leigh Masters, had no interest in dukes, eligible or otherwise.

That particular afternoon Audra felt as if her front parlor was stuffed full of chattering females. Her younger half sister Cecily sat upon the settee before the hearth, discussing the merits of lace and ruching with her dear friend Phoebe Coleby.

Phoebe's mama had stationed herself near the tea caddy on the parlor table, Lady Sophia Coleby's heavy perfume at war with the young ladies' rose-water, tickling Audra's nose, making her want to sneeze. She inched open the long window leading out into the frost-blighted garden and took a bracing gulp of the cold fresh air before returning to her task of pouring out the tea.

Sophia Coleby talked on while reaching for the plate of tea cakes. Her plump, beringed fingers closed about her third, as she scarce missed a stroke in her endless flow of words. "And when the Vicar told me that the Duke of Raeburn had returned, bringing with him his sister and twenty trunks, I was never more astonished in my life. You could have knocked me down with a feather."

"Indeed," Audra murmured, smiling faintly. Feathers be hanged. Nothing less than a battering ram would serve to dislodge Lady Coleby, especially when she was ensconced in someone's parlor for what she termed a "long, comfortable prose."

Audra had long since lost the thread of Lady Coleby's somewhat erratic conversation. Usually she could summon more toleration for her visitor's volubility, but her ladyship would choose today of all days to pay a call. Audra had recently acquired the latest work by the author of the Waverly novels. Even now the second volume of *Ivanhoe* lay nearby upon the caned surface of a Hepplewhite chair, obscured from view by a soft cushion.

She had been lost for hours in a far different world of banished knights, tournaments, and besieged castles. It was very difficult to drag herself back to the clatter of tea cups and Lady Coleby.

When the rap had come at her front door, Audra would have simply denied she was at home, but her seventeen-year-old sister Cecily had fairly leaped to admit Lady Coleby and her eldest daughter. Now Cecily (the little traitoress) had dragged Phoebe off to look at dress patterns, leaving Audra entirely to the mercy of Lady Coleby's loquaciousness. Tucking away a stray tendril of her chestnut-colored hair, Audra resisted the temptation to pull her spinster's cap further down over her ears. Lady Coleby talked on. She never seemed to need to pause for breath, only an occasional sip of tea.

Wistfully, Audra's gaze traveled to where her book lay concealed. She could not resist shifting it

17

onto her lap and opening it to where she had marked her page. Surely it could do no harm to read just a few more paragraphs. All she need do was continue to smile and nod. It would never occur to her ladyship that Audra was not hanging upon her every word.

Audra had discovered that it was possible with many of her callers to read and appear the perfect hostess at the same time. She supposed she ought to be ashamed of herself and was likely to be embarrassed if she was ever caught out. But at the age of eight and twenty, she had come to regard with a cynical eye some of the views of the world.

In others such behavior as hiding books in the folds of her skirts beneath the table might be considered intolerably rude. In a wealthy spinster such as herself, it would merely be termed charmingly eccentric.

Lady Coleby droned on, her voice as soothingly monotonous as the crisp breeze rustling the chintz curtains. Turning another page, Audra eagerly pursued the perils of the beautiful Jewess Rebecca as she tried to repulse the advances of the lustful Bois-Guilbert.

That, reflected Audra, was one problem she had never had. As tall as many gentlemen of her acquaintance, Audra had a trick of looking them straight in the eye in such a manner as to quell even the boldest heart. Nor did she possess such a degree of beauty as to make a man so far forget himself. Her nose was a little too straight, her face a little too angular. With her prominent cheekbones and heart-shaped chin, she possessed none of that dimpled plumpness the gentlemen seemed to find so attractive.

She had been told frequently that her best feature was her eyes, with their thick-fringed lashes and deep gray coloring. During her one Season in London, a young admirer had actually gone so far as to write an ode to her eyes, comparing them to the mists of London. When Audra had tartly asked whether he referred to the fog or the coal smoke, that had mercifully nipped all further poetical offerings in the bud.

With so limited experience in inspiring unbridled passion, Audra refrained from passing judgment on the way Rebecca dealt with the ardent villain. Threatening to leap from the castle walls seemed a little extreme, but Audra could not help admiring Rebecca's calm determination and courage.

It was incredible that the hero, Ivanhoe, should prefer that blond ninnyhammer Lady Rowena to Rebecca's fire and intelligence. The lovely dark-haired Jewess seemed so much more suited to the bold knight.

"One hardly dares to hope for such a thing, but it would make an excellent match, don't you think so, Miss Masters?"

Engrossed in the book, it scarce surprised Audra when Lady Coleby's voice penetrated her haze, the woman in apparent agreement with her.

"Yes, it would," Audra murmured. "Though I suppose there could be some objection on the score of religion."

Lady Coleby gave a startled gasp, setting her tea cup down with a loud clatter. "My dear Miss Masters, I know the Duke of Raeburn has traveled forever in heathen lands, but I daresay he is as devout a member of the Church of England as the next man."

Audra, wrenching her eyes from the book, slowly raised her head like someone surfacing through a sea of confusion, aware of one thing only, that she had just made some remarkable blunder.

Lady Coleby leaned forward conspiratorially, the plumes on her poke bonnet fluttering. "Unless, my dear, you have heard something to the contrary about His Grace? You may tell me. I wouldn't repeat it to a soul."

"Wh-why no," Audra stammered. "I haven't heard—that is I don't even know the man."

"Of course, you do," Lady Coleby said reproachfully. "He is your landlord."

"I *know* that. I meant that I had never met him." When Audra had taken the lease upon Meadow Lane Lodge two years earlier, all the details had been handled by the duke's estate agent, His Grace himself was traveling abroad. The only interest the duke had ever aroused in her was a pang of envy of anyone who had the freedom to travel so extensively and reportedly to such exciting places, Greece, Rome, Egypt. . . . There was much to be said for having been born a man, Audra often thought.

Since she had no idea how she came to be discussing the duke with Lady Coleby, Audra decided that she had best pay a little more heed to her ladyship's conversation. Suppressing a sigh, she nudged her book closed and reached dutifully across the table to refill her guest's cup.

"You must be thinking me the most foolish old woman," Lady Coleby gushed, "to be running on about the duke in this fashion."

"Not at all, ma'am," Audra said politely.

" 'Tis simply the most exciting news I've had in

an age. Everyone in the entire countryside is agog."

Everyone but herself, Audra thought. But that was not unusual. Forever buried among her books, she could name to the day what had occurred in Tudor England, but she never seemed to know what had happened in the neighboring village of Haworth Green just last week.

It was on the tip of her tongue to ask Lady Coleby just what was so exciting when it occurred to Audra that very likely that was what her ladyship had been relating for the past quarter hour. Despite a niggling of curiosity, Audra swallowed the awkward question.

It scarce mattered in any case, for in her usual quicksilver fashion, her ladyship's attention had already shifted direction. Nodding toward the opposite end of the room where Cecily and Phoebe were giggling over some new frock design, Lady Coleby trilled, "Don't our girls present a charming picture?"

Audra swiveled around to observe the two young women settled upon the sofa, Phoebe's dark curls an excellent foil for Cecily's honey-blond tresses. With their heads bent together over the pattern book, and Cecily's foolish little pug curled up between them, twitching its corkscrew tail, they did indeed make a pretty picture.

"How becoming that frock is to your sister," Lady Coleby said. "Quite in the latest mode."

"Very fashionable," Audra agreed, but she caught herself frowning. The sprigged muslin, a confection of lace, and the embroidered trim were wholly unsuited for the chilling breath of November as much so as the dainty green kid slippers Cecily had slipped upon her feet. Staring at her

21

sister, Audra was hard put to recognize the madcap little hoyden their mother had bundled off to boarding school two years ago. Although Audra had never taken much stock in her own appearance, she could have been fiercely proud of Cecily's beauty if her sister had not acquired a parcel of missish airs to go along with it. As it was, Audra found herself missing the little scapegrace with smudged frocks and flyaway curls that Audra had looked after in her mother's frequent absence.

When Cecily glanced up from the patterns long enough to feed her pug part of a biscuit, Lady Coleby said frankly, "I would give half my income for Phoebe to have your sister's complexion and those golden curls. Cecily is so lovely. She looks nothing like you."

"I suppose she doesn't."

"Oh . . . oh dear. That is, I didn't mean—"

"It is quite all right, ma'am," Audra said, laughing a little at Lady Coleby's flustered expression. "I understand exactly what you meant. I take more after Mama while Cecily favors her papa, my late stepfather, Mr. Stephen Holt of Dover."

"Indeed? That would have been your dear mother's second husband?"

"Her third," Audra corrected flatly.

"Oh, that's right. I keep forgetting about Lady Arabella's second marriage to that squire from Worcester. But the poor man only lasted two months so I daresay he shouldn't even count."

Audra refrained from informing Lady Coleby rather tartly that it certainly had counted, at least as far as Audra was concerned. It had meant another upheaval in her childhood, another new house, another stranger to call papa. Sometimes she felt as if she had lived under more roofs than an itinerant peddler, and none of them had ever felt like her home.

Coming from any woman other than Lady Coleby, Audra would have presumed such remarks about her mother's marital escapades to be prompted by a sly malice. But she knew her ladyship was merely curious, and who could blame her for that? There were not many like Lady Arabella who had managed to outlive four husbands and then embark upon a fifth marriage, all before the age of fifty. Audra sometimes feared that if Mama lived to a ripe old age, she might manage to outdo even that notorious king, Henry the Eighth, with his six wives.

She did not enjoy discussing her mother and was relieved when Lady Coleby changed the subject. Her ladyship continued to coo over the two young women. "Such prettily behaved girls, your sister and my Phoebe. Your mama did well to send Cecily to that academy. Girls learn so much at a good school."

"Do they?" Cecily had been with Audra a month now at Meadow Lane Lodge, and Audra had yet to see any sign that her sister's mind was stuffed with a vast store of knowledge.

"Oh, certainly," Lady Coleby said. "Phoebe became so clever upon the harp—to say nothing of her prowess with a brush. Only fancy. She learned japanning. There is scarce a stick of furniture in our house that is not adorned with one of her creations, a posy or some woodland creature. Though I must admit her papa was a trifle vexed over the little bears she put on his escritoire."

"I suppose he might be," Audra said with a glimmer of amusement. Sir John Coleby, being the local magistrate, was a gruff no-nonsense sort of fellow. She could well imagine how he must have bellowed to discover his daughter's artwork upon his favorite desk.

But as for herself, Audra thought she might have borne it better if Cecily had gone about wielding a brush, ruining all the furniture. Even that would have been a far more sensible accomplishment than learning to blush, simper, and flutter one's fan.

Despite these stern thoughts, Audra could feel her expression soften as Cecily danced gracefully up from the sofa. She did not even scold when Cecily closed the French doors. Cecily was forever shutting the house up tight lest her pug escape. In vain did Audra point out to her that that was where a dog belonged, out of doors. Cecily was convinced some dreadful fate would befall her pet.

After one final tug to make sure the door was secure, Cecily tripped over to Audra, Phoebe trailing in her wake, the color in both girls' cheeks heightened by excitement. For once Cecily abandoned all affectation, her blue eyes sparkling with childlike enthusiasm.

"Oh, Audra," she said thrusting the pattern book forward. "Do look at this gown. Wouldn't it be just perfect for Phoebe?"

Audra took a peek at the sketch and crinkled her nose. "Too much lace and surely a little too fine for the local assembly."

"I wasn't thinking of it for the assembly, Miss Masters," Phoebe chimed in. "But for the ball."

"Oh? What ball is that?" To Audra, it seemed the most innocent of questions. But she became uncomfortably aware that all three of the other women were staring at her.

"Why, you know. *The* ball," Phoebe said. "The one to be given at Castle Raeburn. Mama and I received our invitation just this morning."

"Just as I have been telling you, my dear," Lady Coleby added.

Cecily, who had caught sight of the book tucked upon Audra's lap, shot her a look of blistering reproach. "You must pardon Audra, your ladyship. She—she is sometimes a little hard of hearing."

"My advancing years, you know," Audra said dryly.

The good-natured Lady Coleby did not appear in the least put out to have to repeat all that she had said and at a slightly louder volume. "And we were so thrilled to receive our invitation. It was an honor we scarce expected."

"My congratulations, ma'am," Audra said, striving to show all the enthusiasm and wonder that appeared to be expected. "So the Scowling Duke is to give a ball. Only fancy that."

"Audra!" Cecily gasped, looking mortified. "You should not call His Grace that."

"Why not? Everyone else does. He scarcely seems like the sort to host any entertainment. And what a shabby affair it is sure to be, a parcel of dancing and no supper until past midnight."

"That's what balls are, Audra," Cecily said in suffocating accents.

"Well, if that is His Grace's notion of amusement, I am sure he is welcome to it."

"Ah, but there is more to this particular ball than mere amusement." Lady Coleby raised both of her finely plucked brows, looking arch. "Mrs. Wright believes the duke is finally hanging out for a wife."

"Mrs. Wright has six unmarried daughters. She thinks every single male under the age of ninety is seeking a bride. And what on earth does a ball have to do with that?"

Lady Coleby exchanged a look with Cecily and Phoebe, all three of them seeming to despair at Audra's obtuseness. Her ladyship kindly set herself to explain, "Why you see, my dear, it appears the duke doesn't care to go to London looking for a wife. Hopefully, by giving this ball, he will find a lady that will suit."

"Isn't it romantic, Audra?" Cecily chimed in.

"It sounds like a perfectly cork-brained notion to me," Audra said. "His Grace must have maggots in his head if he expects to become that well acquainted with anyone in a crowded ballroom."

This forthright speech made Cecily look ready to sink, but Phoebe giggled and Lady Coleby smiled, shaking her finger at Audra, terming her a naughty creature.

"But always so droll." Gathering the ends of her shawl, her ladyship heaved herself to her feet. "I fear we must be going, Phoebe. Your papa will wonder what has become of us."

Audra's heart gave a grateful leap, the pages of her book seeming to call out to her, but she tried to disguise her eagerness. "Must you be going and so soon?" Not allowing her ladyship a chance to reply, she leaped to her feet. "We won't keep you then. I shall ring to have your carriage brought round at once."

No matter how short a stay her callers paid, Audra always insisted their coachman employ the hospitality of her stables. She couldn't abide the notion of horses being kept standing about, waiting upon dilatory human beings.

But in this instance, Audra had allowed herself to forget what a task it could be, sending Lady Coleby upon her way. Even after she was bundled into her shawl, her ladyship remembered at least half a dozen more important things she needed to tell Audra. Then a search had to be commenced to find Lady Coleby's missing reticule. It had become lodged beneath the settee cushion. After that, her ladyship insisted that she must write down instructions for Audra's housekeeper on an infallible new method for getting berry juice out of muslin.

By the time Audra managed to sweep Lady Coleby and Phoebe through her front door, her ladyship's fine bays had been kept pawing in the traces for a full quarter of an hour.

Concealing her fret of impatience, Audra stepped out onto the lane and waved cheerfully as the two ladies were handed into the carriage. "I hope you and Phoebe enjoy yourselves splendidly at the ball," she called. "You must drop round for tea again very soon."

With Cecily by her side, the two of them continued to wave until the carriage lumbered into motion. As soon as the coach vanished down the lane, Cecily's smile faded and she turned upon Audra a look of pure exasperation.

"Oh, Audra! How could you!"

"How could I what? Invite her ladyship back? It seemed the civil thing to do, and I might as well. She'll come anyway."

"You know that is not what I meant."

As Audra headed back into the house, Cecily trailed after her, still scolding. "I am talking about

27

all those outrageous things you said about the
duke, all those horrid jests, and to Lady Coleby, of
all people. You know what a notorious gossip she
is. Your remarks will be all over the neighborhood
before tomorrow morning."

"Nonsense. Why would she bother talking about
me?" Audra chuckled. "I assure you I am nothing
compared to a duke who travels with twenty
trunks."

She was already dismissing Lady Coleby from
her mind, her thoughts on one thing only. Hastening to the parlor, she found the room odiously stuffy
and managed to inch the long windows open a crack
before Cecily joined her there. With Cecily following her like a small dark cloud, Audra retrieved
her book and mounted a search for her wire-
rimmed spectacles.

"And that is another thing, Audra," Cecily continued to scold. "You have been *reading* again!"

Why did her sister always make that sound as
though Audra had been doing something disrepu-
table, like tying her garter in public? Locating her
glasses, Audra perched them on the bridge of her
nose and peered at Cecily over the rims. "It
wouldn't hurt you to occasionally look between the
covers of a book yourself, miss."

"No, thank you. One bluestocking in the family
is quite enough. You are ruining your eyes. I
quite detest those spectacles you have taken to
wearing and . . . and, oh, Audra, don't you understand? You will get the most dreadful reputation
for oddity."

Audra forbore to remind her sister that she
had had that reputation for years and that Cecily
had never minded it before, at least not until she

had returned from Bath, a graduate of Miss Hudson's Academy for Fashionable Young Ladies.

But she didn't want to quarrel with Cecily again. They seemed to squabble too often of late. Instead Audra chose to ignore her sister's comments, seeking out the sanctuary of her favorite wing-back chair drawn close to the hearth.

She was on the verge of plunking onto it when she was startled by a reproachful yip. Glancing down, she discovered Cecily's pug curled up on the velvet cushion.

"Down!" Audra snapped in a tone of command that would have reduced any of her own hunting dogs to a state of prompt obedience. The pug merely yawned. When she reached out to haul the dog off, the beast emitted a low, menacing growl.

"Audra! You're scaring her," Cecily cried.

"Then have the goodness to remove the little bitch from my chair."

Cecily let out a horrified shriek, but swooped to rescue her pet. Cuddling the dog in her arms, she murmured endearments. "The poor little thing. She's quivering. I've asked you not to shout at her, Audra, or call her anything so horrid."

"But that is what a female dog is called."

"I don't care. It sounds vulgar. Besides she has a name."

"So she does," Audra grumbled as she settled in her chair. "But I could never bring myself to call anything *Frou-frou*."

With an injured sniff, Cecily whisked her dog away as if she feared Audra meant to do the animal some harm, which was ridiculous. Audra was notoriously tenderhearted toward all four-legged creatures, a trait she found slightly embarrassing to admit. She was likely the only person in England who kept a pack of hunting dogs and never hunted. She could not even endure the thought of destroying the vixen who made repeated raids upon her henhouse. Although she could not say that she was fond of Cecily's dog, she would never have wrung its neck, no matter how often she threatened to do so.

After being much petted by Cecily and adjured not to mind "crosspatch Audra," Frou-frou settled into the corner of the settee to resume her nap. Audra, flicking through the pages to where she had left the imperiled Ivanhoe, wished her sister would alight somewhere.

But Cecily hovered over her, hands on hips. "I cannot believe you are going to bury yourself in that book again, especially after we have had such thrilling tidings."

Never glancing up from her volume, Audra searched her memory, but she could recall nothing more thrilling than a complaint from her housekeeper. "I would call it vexing rather than exciting. That is the second time the cow has got into the garden this week. It is all the fault of Sir Ralph Entwhistle and his blasted hunt. If he does not remember to close the gate next time he crosses—"

"Audra! How can you be so provoking! You know I am not talking about any cow or— Do put that book away and pay attention. You never talk to me. I am nigh ready to perish of loneliness."

Audra would have thought that the recent onslaught of Lady Coleby would have been enough to cure anyone of loneliness for a twelvemonth, but she was not proof against the dejected pout of Cecily's lips nor the tiny catch in her voice.

"I am sorry if I have been neglecting you, Muffin," she said, then immediately had to apologize again for letting slip the now-hated childhood nickname.

"For you know I am far too old to be called that anymore, Audra," Cecily said indignantly.

"So you are," Audra said, suppressing a smile and a twinge of wistfulness at the same time. Although she didn't close up the book, she removed her spectacles and reluctantly tried to accord Cecily her full attention.

"What is it you wish to talk about?" she asked, hoping it was nothing to do with the cut of sleeves or the length of hemlines this year. Audra couldn't abide discussing furbelows.

Cecily brightened immediately, sinking gracefully onto the settee opposite. "Why, the ball. The ball to be held at Raeburn Castle. Was there ever anything so delightful?" She did not give Audra a chance to reply but immediately began to enthuse over the pleasures of waltzing in the great hall, sipping champagne, and eating lobster patties. But when she reached the point of wondering at what silk warehouse they should order the material for their gowns, Audra felt obliged to interrupt.

"But Muff—I mean, Cecily, you should not get that excited. There is not the least likelihood we shall be invited."

"Why ever not? After all, your papa was a viscount, and mine was second cousin to an earl. It is not as if we are beneath the duke's touch. I am sure we are every bit as good as the Colebys."

"I never said we were not. What I do say is that His Grace is completely unaware of our existence."

Audra didn't add that if this duke meant to involve them in a foolish round of balls and dinner parties, she was content to remain unknown.

Cecily, however, looked quite crestfallen. "There must be some way of obtaining an introduction," she urged.

"I suppose I could call at the castle and leave my card."

"Oh, no, Audra. You couldn't. A single lady calling upon a gentleman. It simply isn't done."

"Of course, it isn't. Do credit me with some notions of propriety, you goose. I was only funning you."

Cecily glared at her, and Audra sighed. With all the grown-up airs she had acquired, Cecily seemed to have entirely lost her sense of humor. Audra tried to recall if at seventeen *she* had taken everything so deathly serious.

Her brow puckered in thought, after a moment, Cecily asked, "Why can't Uncle Matthew wait upon the duke? I believe he would if you asked him to, Audra."

"Oh, Cecily," Audra said reprovingly and the girl had the grace to blush. The Reverend Matthew Arthur Masters, who was actually Audra's great-uncle, was pushing ninety and rarely ever went into company these days.

"Then I do wish Mama would come home now," Cecily fretted.

Audra tensed as she always did at any mention of their mother. Arabella, the Contessa di Montifiora, was currently traveling through Naples with her fifth husband, on an extended bridal tour. So extended, in fact, that Mama had not been home in over two years. And even if she had, Audra thought somewhat cynically, Lady Arabella would not have been the least use to either one of her daughters. She was too caught up with her own amours. But as Cecily had yet to suffer the same disillusionment with their erratic parent, Audra held her tongue.

Instead, she said, "Missing one ball is not the end of the world, especially this one. I have told you His Grace is likely a most disagreeable man." Audra spoke with a marked authority, although she had only once ever set eyes upon His Grace and that had been a mere glimpse obtained six years ago when she had been fortunate enough to attend the York Races. But she yet retained an impression of a tall, dark-complexioned man with massive shoulders, his thick black brows drawn together in a perpetual scowl.

But Cecily could not be brought to believe that an eligible duke could be other than handsome and charming, the ball to be held at the castle other than a glittering event. The girl's shoulders drooped, and with some trepidation, Audra recognized all the signs of Cecily descending into a state of being absolutely crushed. From there it was only a step away to utterly devastated.

"Never mind, Cecily," she tried to comfort, settling back with her book. "We have other things to look forward to. The strolling players will be returning to Haworth next month, and there is going to be a horse auction at the fair."

To Audra's astonishment, her sister burst into tears. "Oh, Audra, you never understand anything! This place is so h-horridly dull. That ball was the only thing that . . . oh, if I wasn't going to London for my come-out next spring, I-I should simply want

33

to d-die." Upon a final great sob, she stood up and rushed toward the door.

"Cecily! For heaven's sake—" Audra began in exasperation, but her sister had already fled from the room. Audra half started to go after her, but she knew it would do no good. She was a poor hand at consoling Cecily these days. Telling her such bracing things as not to be a widgeon and threatening to dash cold water over her head never seemed to serve the purpose.

"Oh, hang it all. She'll get over it," Audra muttered, flouncing back against the cushions. Cecily's maid would cosset her with cool cloths to the brow and cups of tea, then that would be the end of the matter.

Thus assuring herself, Audra tried to resume her place in the book. But even in the depths of the dungeon at Torquilstone Castle, Ivanhoe in his most dire peril yet, Cecily's unhappy face swam between Audra and the pages. When the bold knight should have been shouting defiance at his enemies, instead he seemed to be mewing, "I simply want to die."

After spending ten minutes trying to read the same paragraph, Audra slammed the book shut in disgust. Rubbing her fingers against her eyes, she wished that the Duke of Raeburn had sunk into the sea before returning home to so cut up their peace at Meadow Lane Lodge.

But she was too honest to entirely blame the present difficulty with Cecily upon the duke. Cecily had been discontent with life at Meadow Lane before Raeburn's return, perhaps even from the moment she had joined Audra there three months ago.

It is so h-horridly dull here. Audra realized Cecily had spoken those words out in pique, and she should ignore them. But the remark stung all the same. Audra had worked very hard to establish a snug, agreeable home for Cecily when the girl should have finished her schooling.

It had never occurred to her that Cecily would dislike Meadow Lane. From the time Audra had first taken the lease, she had found the property perfect, near enough to her Uncle Matthew of whom she was fond, far enough away from other interfering relatives who found it shocking that a spinster should live alone.

Of course, the black-and-white timber lodge was small, having been no more than a hunting retreat. Yet Audra liked the deep masculine tone of the paneled walls. She had scattered about ruby red rugs and hung bright chintz curtains, bringing warmth and light, rendering the house cozy. Here she had enough room for her horses, her dogs, her library. What more could one want?

A companion to share it with, someone whose interests matched her own. The thought came unbidden, but as ever Audra was quick to reject it. She had long ago given up conjuring masculine images in the dark of her room, faces with sympathetic eyes and understanding smiles. And if occasionally she was beset by a peculiar feeling of melancholy or emptiness, she had only to pluck a book from her shelves and bury herself within the pages.

She had been foolish to hope that Cecily would likewise be content with such a reclusive existence. Audra tried to understand, knowing that she was the oddity. Most young women naturally craved the same things Cecily did: society, waltzing balls, handsome suitors.

Perhaps what rendered Audra so frequently irritable and impatient was the realization that she could not give Cecily all those things. Muffin was counting so much upon a London Season. Audra had not as yet found the courage to tell her that she was doomed to disappointment. There would be no coming out for Cecily next Season or perhaps any other. It was not a question of funds, Cecily had inherited a respectable portion and Audra was a considerable heiress in her own right. Audra had to allow her mother that much. Lady Arabella never had thrown her cap over the windmill for a poor man.

The difficulty with Cecily's coming out lay in finding a respectable matron to present her. Audra placed no dependence upon Mama returning to assume the responsibility. The only other likely candidate was Mama's sister. But Aunt Saunders had quite washed her hands of her nieces after the debacle of Audra's own presentation. Audra knew she had been a most reluctant debutante and very difficult, as gawky as a wild colt with her tongue as unbridled as her gait.

When asked her opinion of Almack's, she had replied that she found it very like Tattersall's, only that she thought the horses derived a great deal more amusement at being auctioned off to the highest bidder. Unfortunately, the remark had been overheard by Lady Sefton, one of the all-powerful patronesses of Almack's, resulting in Audra's being denied admittance to those hallowed walls.

Aunt Saunders had been furious. Never had any protégé of hers been refused vouchers. After stigmatizing Audra as a "devil's daughter" in the most icily well bred accents, she had sent her packing and had never spoken to her again, a circumstance Audra had never regretted until now.

That had been over seven years ago, and her aunt still seemed to be holding a grudge. Shortly after Cecily's return from school, Audra had swallowed her own pride and had written a letter upon Cecily's behalf, pleading with her aunt to present Cecily the following spring. Aunt Saunders had not even deigned to reply.

Audra did not know what more she could do. She had never found the charge of her sister a burden before, but she had to admit it had been much easier looking after Cecily when all her hurts could be healed with sticking plaster, all her desires satisfed by an extra cake at teatime.

"You grew up entirely too fast, Muffin," Audra said with a melancholy sigh. But there was no use dwelling on that or she would end by becoming as blue-deviled as Cecily.

Reopening her book, she made one more effort to seek solace as she always did and put the recent frustrating scene with Cecily out of her mind. But she met with no more success than before, being interrupted this time by her housekeeper.

The dour Mrs. McGuiness thrust her head inside the parlor to announce that one of Miss Cecily's suitors, "that there Mr. Gilmore," had stopped by with some posies for her.

Audra grimaced. Until Cecily's arrival, she had never realized so many callow youths inhabited the county.

"Tell him Miss Cecily is indisposed," Audra replied.

"Very good, Miss Audra." Before ducking out again, the housekeeper added, "You might also want to know Jack Coachman said he saw Miss Cecily's dog running off, a-heading for Raeburn's Wood."

"Jack Coachman needs spectacles. Miss Cecily's dog is right over—" Audra began to point toward the settee, but froze in midgesture. The settee was empty.

Mrs. McGuiness clicked her tongue with the usual relish she seemed to take in any impending disaster. "Miss Cecily will be that upset," she predicted with dark satisfaction before bustling off to dispose of the suitor.

Ignoring the woman's grim comment, Audra leaped up, convinced that she would find the little beast still lurking somewhere beneath the furniture, ready to growl at her again.

But she looked under all the chairs without finding any sign of the pug. It was then that her gaze fell upon the window that she had cracked open earlier. With a sinking heart, she saw that it had been shoved much wider than she had left it.

"Oh, blast and perdition!" Stomping through the long window into the garden herself, she placed her fingers to her lips and emitted a series of unladylike but expert whistles.

Of course, there was no response. Audra prepared to retreat to the house, shrugging her shoulders. Surely the little bitch could not be so stupid as to be unable to find her way back home.

Yet uneasily she recalled the report of Jack Coachman. The pug had been seen heading for Raeburn's Wood. It might easily become confused or worse. It might encounter a *real* dog who would make a meal of it.

Audra muttered imprecations under her breath,

but she saw no other remedy. She was going to have to go look for the foolish beast. Cecily was distressed enough already. Audra could hardly face her over the supper table and inform her that her beloved Frou-frou had gone missing.

Pausing only long enough to snatch up her old crimson shawl and a leash, Audra bolted through her front door and down the steps. In her haste, she nearly collided with the young gentleman who lingered in the lane.

Mr. Gilmore had yet to take his leave. His cherubic face wistful above his strangling neckcloth, he stood gazing up toward Cecily's window.

Although startled by Audra's sudden appearance, he recovered, sweeping his curly brimmed beaver from his pomaded locks. "Oh, Miss Masters! Good afternoon. I was so distressed to hear that Miss Cecily—"

"Your pardon, sir." Audra thrust him unceremoniously aside, having neither the time nor patience for lovelorn youths at the moment. "I cannot stop now. The little bitch has escaped. I have to haul her back by the scruff of her neck."

Audra rushed on, oblivious to Mr. Gilmore's open-mouthed expression. He followed her progress down the lane, slowly returning his hat to his head. He had heard stories about the eccentric Miss Masters, how stern she could be, even cruel to her younger sister, but he hadn't credited a word of it. Now he could see plainly those tales were all too true.

CHAPTER 3

Several hours later, Audra tramped along the lane skirting Raeburn's Wood, dried leaves crunching beneath her feet. She had lost both her lace cap and her temper, but was no nearer to recovering Cecily's wretched dog.

Clenching the leash tight in her fist, she muttered, "When I get my hands upon that little bitch, I'll wrap this about her throat." But beneath this fierce threat was a growing sense of unease. The pug had never strayed this far afield before.

When her continued whistles and calls met with no response, she was almost on the verge of doubling back when she heard an answering bark. But such a deep baying could hardly come from Cecily's dog.

While she hesitated, listening, any doubts she may have had were put to rest. Rounding the turn in the lane came two sleek hounds with plumed tails waving. The beasts were hard followed by a rider, a short stocky man mounted upon a gray hunter.

Audra stiffened, having no difficulty in recognizing the local master of the hunt. Sir Ralph Entwhistle was as notorious for his poor seat as for his unruly pack of dogs. Audra had an urge to dive for cover, but it was already too late.

Sir Ralph had spotted her; and man, horse, and dogs bore down upon her at full cry.

"Miss Masters! Huick halloa!"

Audra could never decide what annoyed her most, the way he always greeted her as if she were a vixen on the run or his loud, braying laugh.

She skirted back as he reined his sweating mount close beside her, his dogs barking and leaping at her frock with their muddied paws.

"Here, now. Ratterer! Bellman! Down." When the dogs failed to obey his command, he slashed out with his whip. Audra emitted a horrified protest, but the hounds were already slinking away.

Beaming, Sir Ralph tipped his tall hunter's hat, revealing carroty waves of hair, his bluff features nearly the same shade of red.

"G'day Miss Masters. What're you doin' afoot? Lose your horse?" The baronet guffawed at his own wit.

"No! But I fear you are about to lose yours." She reached up to stroke the nose of Entwhistle's hunter, the beast lathered with sweat, obviously badly winded. She exclaimed indignantly, "Fie upon you, sir. You have nearly ridden this poor creature into the ground."

"Not this lazy brute. I but showed him a good run. Oh, but we had excellent sport today, Miss Masters. Cub hunting. You should have seen it."

"What I did see was my cow, wandering loose. You left my gate open again when you crossed my land."

"Pish!" Sir Ralph dismissed her complaint with a

wave of his hand. "Forget about the cursed cow. I keep telling you, you ought to ride out with the hunt one morning. Exhilarating! Nothing like it. Many wenches do so nowadays."

"Wenches, certainly, but not ladies."

"Bah! I thought you'd a bit more of a dash than to be bothered by any stuffy notions of propriety. B'gawd, madam. I've seen you ride. Good seat, light hands."

"Unfortunately, I cannot return the compliment." Upon further inspection of Sir Ralph's horse, she was nigh sickened to see how the creature's mouth had been ruined by the way he jabbed at the reins.

"Even a performing monkey could be trained to ride better than you," she said. She was a little appalled by her own bluntness, but Sir Ralph only roared with laughter.

"Ha, Miss Masters! What a complete hand you are. Always jesting."

Audra stepped back, pursing her lips. She might have known that it was impossible to insult anyone with a head thicker than last Sunday's pudding. Feeling that she had already allowed him to distract her long enough, she said, "If you will excuse me, sir. I am on rather an important errand."

"I know. I noticed the leash. Searching for Miss Cecily's dog, aren't you?"

Something in Sir Ralph's grin rendered her uneasy. "Why, yes. You haven't by any chance seen it?"

"Dashed well believe I did. Mistook it for a rabbit and set my hounds after it."

Audra felt herself go pale. "You what!"

Sir Ralph shook with chuckles. "Never thought one of those little lap dogs could move so fast. Streaked off into that thicket yonder like a bolt of lightning."

Biting back a curse, Audra whirled in the direction he pointed. "Best make haste, ma'am. That little cur is likely halfway to London by now."

"Why didn't you tell me so at once, you . . . you . . ." But before Audra could think of an epithet strong enough, Sir Ralph emitted another of his donkeylike brays, slashed at his horse, and galloped off, his hounds tearing after him.

Seething with frustrated rage, Audra could only glower at his retreating form. She was angered enough to wish the earth would be rent asunder and send that heedless dolt to the devil—that is as long as the dogs and horse could make it to safety.

But she had little time to waste cursing Sir Ralph. Hiking up her skirts, she raced toward the spot where the baronet claimed to have last seen Cecily's dog. Audra plunged deep into the thicket herself. Sharp twigs scratched her hands and one low-lying branch tangled in her hair.

Pausing long enough to free the stray tendril, she consigned Sir Ralph to perdition. He and his galumphing hounds had made her task thrice as difficult. Cecily's poor pug could be cowering anywhere, by now too terrified to even respond to Audra's calls.

Yet she kept pausing to whistle, kept struggling forward. She figured she must have come better than five miles all told. An indefatigable walker, the distance itself did not bother her, but she viewed with dread the sun sinking lower behind

the trees. Raeburn's Wood was not exactly an un-
tamed forest, but it was no place to wander after
dark either.

Yet the alternative was unthinkable. How could
she return to Cecily without the dog? Perhaps,
though, she should at least work her way back to
the lane. While she was pondering this course of
action, a sound carried to Audra's ear above the
evening song of the lark.

She tensed, listening. It was the bark of a dog
and not the full-blooded cry of anyone's hunting
hound this time. No, such a disagreeable yipping
could only come from Cecily's pug. Audra hesitated
only long enough to determine the exact direction
of the sound, then charged after it.

Shoving branches aside, Audra made her way
forward. Her head bent down, she was in nowise
prepared to suddenly break free into a clearing.
Stumbling a little, she gazed upward and caught
her breath.

The Castle Raeburn itself loomed before her,
those turrets of white stone bathed in the last
golden light of the dying sun. Never having been so
close to the castle before, Audra could only stare. It
was like something out of Ivanhoe or a faery story.
The crenellated battlements, the arched, leaded-
glass windows, the whimsical cone-capped towers
all shimmered in the murky waters of the moat.

Tendrils of ivy crept up the walls, giving the impression of a place abandoned to the mists of time.
Almost unnaturally silent at the twilight hour, the
castle conveyed an aura of enchantment, whispers
of a most delicious danger to any foolish enough to
invade its mystical circle. Although generally not

given to romantic fancies, even Audra hesitated to take a step nearer.

But the spell was broken by the sight of Cecily's pug scampering alongside the moat, growling. Far from appearing overcome by her recent encounter with Sir Ralph's hounds, the idiotic dog was harrying one of the majestic swans swimming past the bank. The creature arched its long white neck, beat its wings, and hissed.

Relief to find the pug unharmed mingled with a sharp sense of irritation. Her reluctance to trespass forgotten, Audra rushed forward, covering the dozen yards or so between herself and the dog. Too late did it occur to Audra that she should have approached with more caution.

Spying her, the leash in her hand, the pug made a break for it, taking refuge beneath a clump of thick bushes along the moat's edge.

Audra swore and began snapping off twigs as she fought to part the branches. "Come out of there, you little—"

Barely she managed to curb her temper, realizing that her angry tone of voice was only making the situation worse. The pug crouched deeper beneath the bush, growling at her. Audra hunkered down. Although the thought made her nigh ill, she knew she would never be able to coax the dog out unless she employed Cecily's manner and made her voice sticky sweet with endearments.

Gritting her teeth, Audra managed to coo, "Come here, darling. That's right. Come on out to me, sweetheart."

"I appear to already be out, madam."

Audra started, momentarily disconcerted by the

deep male voice that seemed to issue from the dog. Then she heard a footstep from behind, a large shadow falling over her. Audra rocked back on her heels, nigh losing her balance. She put her hand down on a sturdy boot, the rolled-down tops besmattered with mud. Yanking her fingers back as if she had just touched a snake, her gaze locked on a pair of well-honed thighs encased in tight buckskin breeches.

Her dismay only deepened as she look upward and found herself kneeling as if in homage to a tall, powerfully built man, his silver-flecked temples emphasizing the night blackness of his hair, his dark eyes boring into her.

For a moment she couldn't move, could scarce breathe. She could not have felt more discomposed than if she had conjured up some black-hearted wizard, the genie who guarded the castle, and he looked about to reduce her to cinders with one flick of his mighty hand.

Those harsh, leathery features, that hawklike profile she had glimpsed only once before, many years ago. But it astonished her how well she recalled his face. The Scowling Duke. Only his frown was much more formidable than she remembered. Even after hearing Lady Coleby's lengthy account of His Grace's return from abroad, it was still unnerving to have him spring up so suddenly before her.

When Audra found her tongue, she blurted out, "Where the deuce did you come from?"

"I was about to ask you the same thing." Placing one gloved hand beneath her elbow, he hauled her none too gently to her feet.

Vague thoughts chased through Audra's brain of

the proper way to greet a duke and she knew full well that had not been it.

"Your Grace, I beg your pardon," she faltered, hoping that despite the fearsome expression, he might prove gallant enough to help her through what was a most awkward moment.

He wasn't.

"Your Grace?" he mocked. "I thought I was your darling."

If there was anything Audra hated, it was to blush, but there was no willing down the hot tide of color that surged into her cheeks.

"Of course you must know I was not addressing you. I was—" She nearly choked to admit it. "I was talking to the dog."

"Dog?" His heavy black brows arched upward, his voice patent with disbelief.

"Yes, a small brown pug. She ran off. She's hiding right over there in those bushes."

Far from appearing convinced, the duke continued to regard her as if she had come to pinch his silverplate. Self-consciously, Audra smoothed back her hair, supposing that in her current disheveled state, she must look far from respectable. Anxious to prove her tale, she bent down and began parting the branches.

"See? The dog's right down . . ." Her voice trailed off as for the second time that day Cecily's despicable dog was not where she should have been. Nothing lurked beneath the bushes but a scattering of fallen leaves.

"She *was* there only a moment ago," Audra said desperately, unable to meet Raeburn's skeptical gaze. She began to stalk up and down whistling, beating the bushes, even going so far as to peer into

47

the moat. All the while she was miserably conscious of Raeburn watching her every move, his arms folded across his chest in a posture of strained patience. As if he had indeed been a sorcerer conjuring his own sudden appearance, he seemed to have caused the dog to vanish as well.

"Damnation!" Audra exclaimed, frustrated beyond endurance. "Now I shall have to begin searching for her all over again. If you hadn't distracted me—" She bit her tongue, trying to recall whom it was she addressed. But Raeburn did not appear offended so much as disgusted.

"A creditable performance, madam," he snapped, "but I don't intend to spend the rest of my evening watching you hunt for a dog that has no existence outside of your imagination. Now what the devil are you really doing here?"

"I *told* you," Audra said crossly, still scanning the line of the woods for some sign of the pug. "And if you don't mind, Your Grace, I am not accustomed to being sworn at."

"No? You swore at me first," he reminded her. He stepped in front of her, the implacable wall of his shoulders blocking her line of vision. Until that moment, Audra had not fully appreciated how tall or how intimidating a figure His Grace could be.

She hated the way her pulse fluttered, her cowardly urge to retreat. She had never been a pudding heart before and wasn't about to begin now. Refusing to yield an inch, she gazed defiantly up him, although the front of her bodice nigh grazed against his waistcoat.

"Whatever your excuse for being here," he said, "I fear you are too late. All the invitations have gone out."

"Invitations?" Audra frowned. Talking to this man was worse than trying to follow one of Lady Coleby's conversations. "Invitations to what?"

"Doing it rather too brown, my dear. I am talking about the ball, as you well know."

"Oh, *that*. Yes, I had heard something about it."

"I'll wager you have. Well, I congratulate you, Miss . . ."

"Miss Audra Leigh Masters of Meadow—" Audra began, then stopped, thinking it perhaps less than wise to inform His Grace she was his tenant. In his present ill humor, he might be likely to evict her.

"Miss Masters, your approach is a little more original than the others. At least I have not had to endure your swooning or pulling your horse up lame."

"I never faint. I take excellent care of my horses and . . . and I haven't the vaguest notion what you are talking about."

"Take care, madam," he growled. "You have already tried my patience to its limits. I assure you I have been beset all week by *ladies* such as yourself. Apparently the word has gone out there is a vacancy here for the post of duchess. Since you have gone to such effort, I suppose I should give you due consideration."

Before Audra could react, he seized her by the chin and forced her head up. Studying her through narrowed eyes, he murmured, "Hair, tolerable, although it could use a thorough brushing. Teeth appear to be good, eyes an unremarkable gray." His gaze dipped in a quick appraisal of her figure. "Rather a Long Meg, but I like that. I get tired of stooping down to talk to people."

Momentarily dumbfounded, Audra could only stare at him. She had heard tell the duke was a disagreeable man, but it had never been bruited about that he was quite mad. As the full import of his accusations finally sank in, she gave vent to an outraged gasp, striking his hand away.

"You think that . . . that I only pretended to . . . that I came here a-purpose to seek you out so . . . Why, you . . . you are the most despicable coxcomb I ever met, or else a raving lunatic. Let me tell you, sir, if I was in the market for a duke, I would scarce be searching for one beneath the shrubberies, while carrying a leash."

Although he continued to regard her with that infuriatingly sardonic expression, a shadow of uncertainty flickered in his eyes.

Trembling, Audra could scarce find words adequate to express her indignation. "I-I am a spinster, Your Grace, and fiercely proud of it. I have a fortune of ten thousand pounds a year, a stable with several fine horses, and a kennel full of dogs. I do not need a husband."

"I beg your pardon," he drawled.

"So you should. And furthermore, even if you had sent me an invitation, I would not come. Neither I nor my sister have any interest in attending your odious ball." Audra considered what Cecily's reaction would be if she were privileged to hear Audra saying such a thing, but in her present anger, Audra gave it no more than a fleeting thought. She finished up by loftily informing the duke, "I wouldn't come to that ball even if you got down on one knee and begged."

The stern set of his mouth twitched with something akin to amusement. "Since there is little likelihood of my doing that, I fear I will be deprived of the pleasure of your fair company."

Audra glared at him. "You have to be the most conceited person I have ever met. But there! What more can be expected of a man who travels with twenty trunks full of clothes?"

He looked a little confounded at that, and feeling as if she had at least gotten a little of her own back, Audra started to flounce away from him when she caught sight of a movement by the edge of the woods. Cecily's pug darted into sight, this time in fierce pursuit of a frog. Feeling vindicated, Audra could not refrain from flashing the duke a look of triumph.

"If Your Grace will excuse me, I must see about recovering my imaginary dog."

But she had not taken two steps nearer to the little beast when, as usual, the pug began to growl and back away as if it had never set eyes upon Audra before. A peculiar choked sound came from the duke's direction. If it had been anybody else but Raeburn, Audra would have sworn the man smothered a laugh.

"Come here, Frou-frou," she called through clenched teeth.

"Frou-frou?" the duke echoed. His Grace might not know how to smile, but he certainly could smirk.

"I assure you I never named her that," Audra began hotly, then broke off. What was the use? It was a complete waste of time trying to explain anything to that man. Besides, with a jaunty flick of its tail, the pug was racing back into the woods again. Audra charged after it, not even troubling to bid the duke farewell.

Raeburn watched as both the pug and the woman vanished into the twilight, leaving the glade behind his castle seeming strangely deserted. A rueful half smile escaped him. He scarce knew whether to laugh or curse, his amusement tempered by an uncomfortable feeling that he had just made a thorough ass of himself.

"How was I to know there really was a dog?" he muttered. It was all the fault of Miss Long and her scheming kind, their foolish stratagems rendering him suspicious of any woman he chanced upon. He had never before been wont to think that every stray female was eager to cast herself into his arms.

Even if he had, Miss Masters had certainly set him straight on that score. Simon did laugh then, as he recalled the lady's indignation when she had informed him she had no use for a husband. She had looked rather magnificent, that wild mane of chestnut hair tumbling about her shoulders, her eyes flashing scorn. Not a beauty by any means, but he had lied when he had said her eyes were unremarkable. Far from it, he thought they were the most honest gray he had ever seen.

He supposed he ought to set off after Miss Masters and tender her some explanation of his boorish conduct, even extend an apology. But he had too great a regard for his own nose. In her present humor, the lady was likely to draw his cork. Besides he doubted he would catch up to her, and he had no notion where she lived.

Simon shrugged, telling himself it was of no great consequence. He hardly need worry about currying the good opinion of a woman he'd scarce met and one moreover he was unlikely ever to see again. Dismissing the incident from his mind, he followed the line of the moat, heading for the wooden bridge that crossed to the inner court of the castle.

He returned to his bedchamber to change for dinner, as they kept country hours at the Castle Raeburn. While he struggled into a fresh white shirt, he was surprised to find himself still thinking about Miss Masters, recalling some of the things she had said to him. What was it she had called him? The most conceited person she had ever met, but then what more could be expected of a man who traveled with twenty trunks?

Simon frowned, wishing he had informed her that nineteen of those twenty trunks she had spoken of belonged to his sister. But then, what business was that of Miss Masters? Still it irked him all the same, he who prided himself on his good sense and the plain manner of his attire, being accused of being a popinjay.

He could not help brooding about it as he descended belowstairs to lead Lady Augusta into the dining room. Was Miss Masters partly correct? Not about the trunks, of course, but about his conceit. Had he become a little too puffed up of late, too full of his own consequence as the duke?

Annoyed with himself for giving any weight at all to what Audra Masters had said, Simon attempted to shake off his air of abstraction. Linking his arm through Augusta's, he led her into the small dining chamber. Simon much preferred its simple paneled walls to the more ostentatious formal one with its gilt and trim and overwhelming chandeliers.

Waving aside the footman, he held the chair for Augusta himself and then settled at the opposite end of the gleaming satinwood table.

During the course of turtle soup, Augusta made cheery inquiry as to how his walk had gone. "You were absent so long. I am sure you could not have spent all that time just looking at a bull. What did you do with yourself all afternoon?"

"Nothing of import, merely made a fool of myself."

"Oh." Augusta took a spoonful of creamy broth. "I thought you might have done something different for a change."

He accorded this sally no response. He considered regaling Augusta with his encounter with Miss Masters but thought better of it. Gus had already enjoyed enough mirth at his expense for one day.

Instead he could not refrain from asking abruptly, "Gus, do you find me conceited?"

"No, dear. Only impossibly arrogant."

Simon grimaced. Trust a sister to provide all the reassurance one needed.

Augusta looked up from her soup dish, regarding him with a puzzled look. "Whatever makes you ask such a thing?"

"No particular reason." Simon was quick to change the subject, asking how the preparations for the ball were going.

It served the trick of diverting Augusta's thoughts, but he was almost sorry. She launched into a lengthy account of her concerns about acquiring enough lobster.

"And I still cannot make up my mind how to decorate the ballroom," she lamented. "Would simple floral arrangements be enough, or should I try for something more exotic?"

"Hanging the room with black crepe seems appropriate." His suggestion met with no more than a disgusted look from his sister.

Even though he had inquired, Gus ought to realize all these details about the ball did not interest him in the least. Not a single aspect of it except perhaps . . .

To his own astonishment, Simon caught himself asking, "Have you sent out all the invitation cards?"

"Of course. But if you have recollected someone else you wish to invite, I suppose—"

"Oh, no. No!" Simon made haste to disclaim. A vision of Audra Leigh Masters danced through his mind, only to be quickly dismissed. "Why the blazes should I want any more infernal females invited?"

"Well, I did think we might have asked the Marquess of Greenwold. He has two charming daughters, though they do live a little far off."

"Then no matter how charming, let them stay there. I don't want to be plagued with any overnight guests." Clearly bored with the subject, Simon summoned a footman to refill his wineglass.

"You might show a little more concern, Simon," Augusta complained. "At least in what ladies will be in attendance."

"Why? I fear that the only female that has roused even a passing interest in me, has already said she'll be damned if she's coming."

"What!" Startled, Augusta dropped her fork, clattering it against her dish. "Simon! Who is she?"

But Simon already looked as if he regretted having said so much. He attacked a joint of lamb instead, maintaining a most maddening silence. Augusta knew that stubborn look too well to badger him with any more questions. Consumed with curiosity, her own dinner went untasted, and she glowered at him. If she did not murder her brother before this visit was over, it would not be because he hadn't done his utmost to goad her to it.

CHAPTER 4

For several days after her encounter with the Duke of Raeburn, Audra's thoughts still turned on all the crushing retorts she should have uttered. The arrogance of that man! That he should have supposed for one minute that she had come creeping about his estate, merely to throw herself at his head, assuming that she was like all these other foolish chits hereabouts, panting to make his acquaintance.

Audra's cheeks burned anew whenever she recalled the duke's insolent manner, subjecting her to his inspection. Had she been a vain woman, she would have been quite devastated by some of his remarks about her person. A Long Meg with unremarkable eyes indeed! She was fully aware of her own defects and did not need them pointed out.

Although she had given him a blistering scold, she had not said near enough. This frustrating feeling was coupled with a dread that she had said perhaps too much. Apparently he had not realized she was his tenant, but there was no saying that he wouldn't by now since she had so stupidly furnished him with her name. She did not know if His Grace was a vindictive man, but he obviously had a formidable temper. She lived with the hourly expectation of a notice arriving, demanding her immediate eviction from Meadow Lane.

Yet she doubted she need fear any such grim messenger today. Rain was coming down so hard, one would have to be a madman to venture forth. Water cascaded down the long windows in the parlor like a waterfall. Audra regretted the fact she had invited her great-uncle Matthew to travel from his home in the village to spend the day with her and Cecily. She hoped that elderly gentleman would have the good sense to send his excuses.

But her relative seemed short of that commodity, for shortly after noon Mrs. McGuiness popped her head into the parlor to announce that the Reverend Masters's carriage was fair floating down the lane. Biting back a dismayed exclamation, Audra joined the housekeeper at the front door to hustle her uncle inside, helping the plump elderly gentleman to remove his drenched cape and rain-slicked beaver hat.

His flowing waves of white hair were pulled back into a slightly bedraggled queue. Beneath brows as thick as a drift of snow, his pale blue eyes twinkled up at Audra.

"Stap me, m'dear, but I believe I should have brought my oars."

"Uncle, you are fair drowned," Audra said. "Come by the fire at once."

"Don't fuss, girl." Reverend Masters paused to chuckle and pat the round belly straining beneath his waistcoat. "'A man of my girth is hardly like to be washed away."

Nonetheless he permitted himself to be led to the chair before the parlor hearth. His cherub's face glowed from the heat of the crackling blaze, his complexion remarkably smooth for a man of ninety-odd years. It was hard for Audra to remember sometimes that he had been her father's uncle, not her own. Reverend Masters attributed his longevity to the fact he had never listened "to a demned thing" the fool doctors told him, always stuffing himself with as much pastry and Madeira as he desired.

"Ah, that's better." He sighed as he held his hands over the blazing fire. His nose turned a bright red as it always did when he was too warm or had drunk too much port.

Although he protested, Audra insisted he remove his boots. As she knelt down before him and tugged them off, she continued to scold. "It isn't that I am not glad to see you, Uncle, but you should never have come out on such a day."

"I had to, m'dear. Another day closeted at the parsonage, and I would be fit for naught but Bedlam. Would you believe it, I was so desperate to fill my hours, I nearly thought of writing a sermon."

Audra laughed, too accustomed to such outrageous comments from her uncle to be shocked. There had never been anyone less suited for holy orders than Matthew. But as he had explained to Audra once, "What the devil else is there for a younger son besides the army? I could tolerate being shot at by some irate husband, but by a total stranger I had done nothing in the least to offend? No, no, m'dear. That is asking entirely too much."

He was something of a reprobate, her uncle Matt, and greatly scandalized the rest of her father's family. Those same fusty relatives did not approve of Audra either, which perhaps was why she and Uncle Matthew got on so famously. Whatever the reason, Audra was immensely fond of the old gentleman. His proximity had proved one of the chief inducements to her signing the lease on the lodge.

Without making her solicitude so obvious as to vex the old man, Audra removed his boots and took great pains to make sure he hadn't taken a chill.

She had just settled upon the settee opposite him when Cecily tripped into the parlor, Frou-frou ambling at her heels.

"Was that Uncle Matt's carriage I heard arriving?"

" 'Deed it was, miss." Uncle Matthew's broad face fairly beamed. "Bless me, the child grows lovelier every day. Come here, my pretty niece, and give your uncle a kiss."

Cecily dutifully complied, bestowing a soft peck on his cheek. Audra watched with tolerant amusement. Although he was not in truth Cecily's uncle, Reverend Masters had "adopted" her, ever having a soft spot in his heart for a lovely girl. Never averse to receiving compliments, Cecily gave him a dazzling smile.

But Audra was forced to admit that Cecily had been nothing but charming these past few days. She had never mentioned a word about their quarrel, her disappointment over having to miss the upcoming ball, or any of her dissatisfaction with life at Meadow Lane. Her disposition had been of such a sweetness, so cheerful, so obliging, it was enough to make one wonder if the girl was up to some mischief.

Yet Audra was immediately ashamed of herself for harboring such a suspicion. She was becoming

as evil-minded as his horridness, the Duke of Raeburn.

Cecily seated herself upon a footstool, near the
arm of Reverend Masters's chair, playfully calling
upon Frou-frou to "make her curtsy to Great-uncle
Matt." The dog actually deigned to wag her tail for
him. It was apparently only Audra at whom the
little beast chose to growl.

That did not disturb Audra, who still felt like
doing some growling herself, every time she recollected how Frou-frou's escapade had led to her disastrous meeting with Raeburn.

It didn't help to hear Cecily merrily regaling Uncle Matt with the story, at least as much of it as she
knew. Giggling, she said, "And naughty Frou-frou
led my sister on quite a chase through Raeburn's
Wood. Poor Audra was out looking for her until
well after dark."

"Oh, brave woman!" Uncle Matt's gaze shifted
toward Audra, clearly taking a wicked relish in her
discomfiture. "What? Were you not afraid of the
Scowling Duke leaping out to demand a forfeit for
your trespass?"

To her dismay, Audra felt a hint of red creep into
her cheeks. Was it possible that Uncle Matthew
had actually heard something of her meeting with
Raeburn? It had never occurred to her that the
duke might be so ungentlemanly as to spread the
tale of their infamous encounter.

Audra squirmed in her seat. "Wh-what makes
you ask me such a thing, Uncle Matt?"

"Nothing, m'dear. 'Twas only a jest, certainly
naught to make you look as if you had just swallowed a fly."

"You will have to excuse me," she said stiffly. "I found the whole affair less than amusing."

"Why, Audra, it's quite unlike you to take snuff over such a trivial thing. What's happened to your sense of humor, child?" Her uncle shot her a puzzled but penetrating look that rendered Audra extremely uncomfortable. She felt relieved when Cecily inadvertently came to her aid by explaining, "I fear Audra has reason to still be cross. While she wore herself to the bone tramping the woods, my wicked little Frou-frou doubled back." Cecily dotingly rubbed her pet's neck. "Audra returned in despair, only to discover Frou-frou curled up in her favorite chair."

Uncle Matt and Cecily both chuckled at that, laughter in which Audra was quite unable to join. She glared at Frou-frou, muttering, "That dog is lucky to still be alive."

"I daresay." Uncle Matt chortled. "Especially knowing you m'dear, I don't doubt but what the search interrupted your reading." The rector reached down to pat an open book that was, as always, left littering the small chairside table. Uncle Matthew squinted at the spine. "Why, by my faith, is this still *Ivanhoe*? I thought you received this book days ago. With your habit of devouring books, you ought to be done and ready to lend it to me."

"I have been a little distracted of late," Audra said. She was not about to admit the distraction was of a most disturbing and curious kind. Poor Ivanhoe was indeed a sorely vexed man with his sweetheart and father held prisoner at Torquilstone. But that was no reason that every time she pictured the knight's scowling face, the image should turn into Raeburn's dark frown. Nor why at the turn of every page, her traitorous mind should keep conjuring up a hero with black, silver-flecked hair and fierce bushy brows. It was not only annoying but foolish to keep imagining Ivanhoe in Raeburn's massive proportions, that deep chest, those broad shoulders, and those brawny forearms. Audra had seen samples of armor before. If Ivanhoe had been such a strapping figure of a man, the metal plating would never have fit him.

Since she quite detested His Grace, she didn't know why Raeburn should assume the role of Ivanhoe in her mind. If he must invade her head, she should imagine him as the blackhearted villain Front de Beouf. Better still she should not think of Raeburn at all.

It disconcerted her to realize that her inability to concentrate had not gone unnoticed, even by Cecily. She informed Uncle Matthew in grave tones, "Audra has been so restless of late. But I suppose that is the sort of crotchets that older, er, I mean that more mature ladies have from time to time."

"No, it's only the damp," Audra retorted. "My rheumatism, you know."

Uncle Matt choked at that, and Audra took the opportunity to change the subject by challenging him to a game of chess. He was a skilled player, and Audra had enjoyed many lively skirmishes with him in the past, neither giving much quarter.

Lining up the ivory pieces upon the board, she and the old gentleman were soon engrossed in the game. The afternoon passed pleasantly enough despite the rain that beat against the glass. The parlor was silent but for an occasional snort from Frou-frou, the crackle of the logs on the fire, the tick of the clock on the mantel.

Even Cecily sat quietly engaged with her stitching. If she was bored, she concealed her occasional yawns behind her hand. Audra lost all track of time, breathlessly watching her uncle's hand hover over his bishop, waiting for him to fall into her trap.

She did not notice when the rain stopped until her sister pointed it out her. Springing up from her seat, Cecily skipped over to the windows.

"The sun is trying to come out. Perhaps there will be a rainbow." Cecily flattened her nose against the glass. "Oh, Audra, do come and see."

Since Uncle Matt had somehow managed to turn the tables upon her and Audra discovered her queen in peril, she was too preoccupied to stir. In any case, Cecily's raptures seemed a little excessive for a bit of colored sky.

"Pray, don't bother me now, Muffin," Audra murmured. "I am sure the rainbow will still be there later."

"It isn't a rainbow. It's a coach and four coming down the drive."

Audra's and the rector's heads jerked up simultaneously. Her own groan was echoed by Uncle Matt.

"If it's that Coleby woman, I warn you, Audra, I'll hide myself in the wine cellar until she's gone."

"Shame on you, uncle," Cecily said. "You are as bad as Audra. It isn't Lady Coleby's carriage at all. It is—" She broke off with a gasp. Retreating a step from the window, she stood pale, transfixed.

"Cecily?"

When Audra received no response to her sharp

inquiry, she became concerned enough to abandon the chessboard and join her sister at the window. "Whatever is the matter, Muffin?"

Too overcome to speak, her eyes round as saucers, Cecily could only pluck at Audra's sleeve and point out the window. Audra looked out and froze, feeling as if she had just turned to stone herself.

Pulling to the front of the cottage was a shiny black coach with a team of gaily caparisoned white horses in the traces. An outrider led the way, blowing upon his trumpet. Emblazoned upon the carriage door was a coat of arms, but the insignia was no more impressive than the coachman, the two footmen who rode behind all garbed in sapphire blue livery.

"Audra," Cecily quavered. "Do you think it is the— the—"

"The devil!" Audra cried. She could not imagine that it was the King of England come to call. Only one person hereabouts was likely to have such a rig-out as that.

"Raeburn!" she said.

Cecily gave a shivery sigh and looked likely to swoon. Audra wanted to shake her sister for being such a goose, but she could scarce do so. Not when her own heart was racing in such idiotic fashion.

Uncle Matthew had obviously not heard her pronouncement for he called out testily, "Are you two girls just going to stand there like stocks or are you going to tell me? Whose coach is it?"

Before Audra could say a word, Cecily trilled out, "It's the duke's carriage, uncle. Isn't it wonderful? Oh, Audra!" Cecily's blond curls bounced with her excitement. "Why do you think His Grace is coming here?"

Audra could imagine several reasons, none of them good. "I don't know," she said glumly. "But perhaps we had best go upstairs and start packing."

"What?!"

Audra ignored her sister's startled exclamation. Not wanting to be spied ogling, she inched further behind the drapes. Holding her breath, she watched one of the footmen spring forward to open the coach door, bracing herself for the sight of that familiar arrogant profile.

But the man who alighted was a stranger to her. Although of distinguished bearing, his garb was simple, marking him as no more than a servant himself. Yet with a great parade of self-consequence, he marched toward the lodge's front door.

"Oh!" Cecily's shoulders slumped with chagrin.

Audra felt she could have echoed that sentiment, but whether from relief or a similar sense of disappointment she refused to consider.

Impatiently, Uncle Matthew stumped over to join them. "What the deuce is t'ward?"

Audra shrugged, being as ignorant as he. But it seemed none of them were to be kept in suspense for long. Whatever errand the duke had sent this man upon, it was discharged promptly. After disappearing from view for a moment during which Audra heard muffled sounds of her front door being answered by Mrs. McGuiness, the duke's man popped into sight again.

Clambering back into the carriage, the coachman whipped up his team, and the impressive entourage departed as suddenly as it had come. Audra caught a last view of the vehicle vanishing down the lane by the time Mrs. McGuiness entered the parlor.

The dour housekeeper appeared a little awed herself as she approached Audra. She bore a missive of some sort upon a silver tray much to Audra's wry amusement. Apparently Mrs. McGuiness had not thought it good enough to hand over a letter from the duke as she always did the regular mail. So she had employed the silver serving tray normally used for holding the tea service.

The housekeeper thrust the tray at Audra, too overcome to say more than, "For you, Miss Masters."

"Thank you." Audra took up the letter gingerly as though it were likely to explode. If it were an eviction notice, never had one been sent so elegantly as this square of creamy vellum with the duke's heavy seal imprinted upon the wax closure. Was it just possible . . . ? No, it seemed utterly incredible to even imagine that the overbearing duke might have penned her an apology.

Whatever the contents of the missive, one thing was certain. She would never find out by simply turning it over and over in her hands. Audra started to break the seal, when she became aware of three heads crowded close to hers. Mrs. McGuiness was the worst, nearly toppling into Audra in her efforts to see.

"Shouldn't you be starting the tea?" Audra asked repressively.

Mrs. McGuiness pursed her lips, but she took the hint, beating a disappointed retreat. Now if only she could be rid of Cecily and her uncle as easily.

At a look from Audra, Uncle Matthew did appear a trifle sheepish and stepped back a pace, but nothing could discourage Cecily from hanging on Audra's sleeve.

"Oh, Audra, do you wish to kill me with this suspense? Do not wait any longer. Open it. Open it!"

Although fearful of what the note contained, Audra broke the seal and unfolded the vellum. She strove so hard to focus on the elegantly inked lines, it took some moments for the sense of the words to sink in.

"*His Grace, the Duke of Raeburn, and Lady Augusta Penrose,*" Audra mused aloud, "*request the honor of your presence at—*"

She got no further for Cecily fairly shrieked in her ear, "At the ball! Audra! It's an invitation to the ball."

Audra stared. When she realized for herself what it was she held in her hands, she dropped the vellum as if her fingers had been scorched. While she stood stunned, Cecily snatched up the invitation.

Waving it wildly over her head, Cecily danced about the room, breathless with joyous laughter. "The ball! Oh, Uncle Matthew, we're going to the ball."

Cecily flung her arms about the rector, causing the old man to laugh with delight himself. He patted her shoulder indulgently, saying, "Are you indeed, my pet?"

Audra had scarce time to brace herself before Cecily rushed wildly at her as well, enveloping her in a crushing hug.

"Oh, Audra, I knew you would find some way to arrange the invitation when I so wished for it. You are the best, kindest, dearest sister in the whole world."

Audra's mind whirled as she struggled to make sense of all of this. Gasping, she eased herself out of Cecily's strangling embrace. "Cecily, do control yourself. This has to be some kind of mistake."

"How could it be?" Cecily waved the invitation before Audra's eyes. "Both of our names are clearly marked." Audra tried to see but Cecily would not stay still long enough for her to get a good look at the blasted thing again.

Audra frowned, knowing full well she had done nothing to secure that invitation. Far from it! If Cecily had any idea of half the things Audra had said to His Grace . . .

So how had their names come to be added to the guest list? Had someone else put in a word on their behalf? Audra glanced toward her uncle with sudden suspicion.

But Uncle Matthew shrugged. "Do not look at me thus, Audra. I had naught to do with it. You know my infernal gout keeps me from getting out as much as I would like. Though long acquainted with the Lakeland family, I have not even seen His Grace since his return."

Nigh delirious with happiness, Cecily continued to frolic about the parlor, her activity causing Frou-frou to yip while Audra wracked her brains for some explanation.

The only one possible was that after meeting her, the duke himself had somehow traced where she lived and discovered the name of her sister. But why, after Audra had insulted him, should he take such pains, sending the invitation when she had sworn to turn it down?

"Plague take the man," she muttered. "He must have sent it just to vex me." Whipping round, she snapped, "Cecily, do cease this unseemly display at once."

Cecily subsided enough for Audra finally to grab the invitation away from her. She crushed it in her hand. "There is no chance whatsoever of our accepting this thing."

Cecily's bright smile faded. Young Juliet could not have looked more stricken when discovering her Romeo was dead.

"Audra! Wh-what are you saying?"

"I'm saying we are not going. It would be . . . wholly improper."

"Improper! I see nothing in the least objectionable in attending. Do you, Uncle Matthew?"

But the Reverend Matthew Masters, sensing a storm about to brew, wisely retreated back to his chessmen, determined not to be caught in the middle.

"It's improper because . . ." Audra groped for some plausible excuse. "Because you are not even out yet."

Cecily's face flushed with indignation. "As if you ever cared for such fustian notions. Besides this is a private ball, not at all like you were taking me to an assembly."

"It is of no avail arguing with me, Cecily. My mind is made up. We are not going because I do not wish to—"

"You never wish to go anywhere," Cecily cried with a stomp of her foot. "You keep both of us cooped up in this dreadful house. It's . . . it's horrid and . . . and wicked of you. My entire life is passing me by."

"What utter nonsense. You are only seventeen."

"I'll be eighteen soon, and before I know where I am at, I'll end up an old maid just like you."

After which passionate speech, Cecily spun on her heel, bolting for the door.

Uncle Matthew sprang to his feet. "Here now, Cecily. What a dreadful thing to say. You come back and apologize—"

The door had already slammed closed behind her.

"Let her go, uncle," Audra said dully. "She's right. I am an old maid, and I don't mind it in the least."

Her voice did not carry its usual conviction though, and she gave vent to a weary sigh. "I suppose Cecily will spend the rest of the afternoon weeping again."

"I fear 'tis all part of being seventeen, m'dear."

"Is it? I don't recall. Sometimes I don't think I ever was that age."

"No, you were never given the chance to be. I always said your mama saddled you with too much responsibility too young. Why doesn't Lady Arabella return to take charge of Cecily?"

Audra shuddered. "Please, don't wish such a thing upon me. More likely I would end up taking care of Mama as well."

She meant it as a jest, but memories crowded forward all the same, assuring her that her words were not far from the truth. Lady Arabella had ever been a flighty creature, given to acquiring herself the most doting, elderly husbands. It had always fallen to Audra's lot to prevent her mother from overspending or creating a scandal with her latest handsome lover.

It might be most unfilial to admit, but she was

71

quite content to have Mama continue her latest bride trip indefinitely. Rousing herself from these disagreeable reflections, Audra moved to chuck the invitation into the fire. She was astonished when Uncle Matthew's hand shot out to prevent it.

Those pale blue eyes, usually so merry, were clouded with trouble. "Don't be so hasty, m'girl. You might want to reconsider attending that ball."

"Uncle!"

Ignoring her exclamation, he continued, "Though I cannot approve of Cecily's manner, behaving like a spoiled child, some of what she said is true. 'Tis not good the way you live here, so much alone. You are a young woman still, Audra."

"Not that young. You have only to ask Cecily. I believe she thinks I am a contemporary of Methusaleh." Audra's wry smile coaxed no like response from him.

"You are not going to commence scolding me, too, are you Uncle Matt?" she asked. "I have heard enough regarding my shocking manner of life from Lord Sunderly."

Indeed, the cousin who had inherited her father's title had thought it the most outrageous thing since the Gunpowder plot, that Audra should set up her own establishment with only a housekeeper for a companion. But since neither Lord Sunderly nor any of Papa's other relatives had ever troubled themselves about Audra's welfare before, she did not feel obliged to regard their disapproval.

But her uncle Matthew had rarely ever lectured her. Consequently Audra found his words not so easy to dismiss. "You know well enough that I never preach propriety, Audra. But a companion would enable you to get out more, receive more people. Heavens, child, you see no one but myself and that Coleby woman. And that is only because no one can keep that dratted chattering female out."

Audra drew herself up proudly. "You mistake, sir, if you think me unhappy. I am quite content with my quiet way of life. My only concern is about Cecily. I know that she should have more gaiety, a Season in London, perhaps."

She lowered her eyes, coming down from her high ropes a bit. "I even wrote my aunt Saunders about it, but unfortunately she has not replied. I suppose she still remembers the debacle I made of my own Season."

"That was scarcely your fault. Your mama never did anything to prepare you. Letting you closet yourself in the schoolroom and without a proper governess to even teach you the way to get on."

Audra rarely felt the urge to defend her mother, but in all fairness, she could not let her own social failure be laid at Arabella's door. "I learned everything I ever wanted to out of my books," she said. "And you can hardly blame Mama for my clumsiness. Even the best of tutors cannot turn a goose into a swan."

Uncle Matt looked as if he wanted to argue that point, but instead he said, "Well, I suppose that's all water under the bridge. It is the future I am worried about. How are you and your sister ever to meet any eligible gentlemen shut away here at Meadow Lane?"

Audra smiled. "We have gentleman callers all the time. Young Sir Worthington, Mr. Gilmore, Mr. Blake. And I play chaperon to Cecily as a proper old-maid sister should."

"And which of those youths do you want Cecily to marry? That silly ass Gilmore or that boy with the spots?"

The question startled Audra. "Why, none of them. They are all but callow boys, scarce out of the nursery."

"Well, you had best brace yourself, m'dear. I fear Cecily is not as strong-minded as you. If she is given no other choice, you are likely to end up with one of those boys for a brother-in-law."

Audra started to hotly refute his prediction, but she found she couldn't. It wasn't as if she didn't want Cecily to have better opportunities.

"I tried to get Muffin a London Season," Audra said. "What more can I do?"

"You could make the most of this." Her uncle tapped the vellum she yet held crushed in her hand. "Give me one good reason, miss, why you and your sister should not attend that ball."

"There are several—" Audra began, but incurably honest, she recognized the chief one, her stiff-necked pride. How could she turn up so humbly on Raeburn's doorstep, after all her expressions of scorn, informing him she would not come if he begged her? The duke would be bound to think her no better than all these other fluttery chits after all. But she could not admit these qualms, not even to Uncle Matt.

She finished lamely, "It would be most uncomfortable, taking Cecily alone, with—with no male escort or older relative to—"

Her uncle puffed out his chest. "What do you take me for—the pantrymaid? It so happens, miss, that as a courtesy, I am always invited to functions at the castle. I had no intention of attending this ball myself, but now I can see where it would be a very good thing."

"Oh, Uncle Matt, Cecily and I couldn't possible drag you off to such a fatiguing affair."

"Fatiguing, be demned. I would quite enjoy it. I am scarce in my dotage yet, miss." His eyes turned suddenly misty with memories. "Faith, it has been a long time since I have stood up with a lady. Did you know that his majesty, that is the late king, poor mad George, once told me I was the most skilled dancer to ever grace St. James?"

"I am sure you were, Uncle." Audra reluctantly smoothed the vellum out again.

His Grace, the Duke of Raeburn requests the honor . . .

Was it possible that the words meant just that? That perhaps instead of being another gibe, this invitation was a peace offering, Raeburn's awkward manner of making amends for his insulting behavior?

As Audra's doubts made her hesitate, Uncle Matthew poured forth the full force of his persuasion, stressing how much social good it would do Cecily, to say nothing of how happy Audra would make him. Audra sighed. The Reverend Matthew Masters did not possess the ability to thunder from the pulpit, but Audra was convinced her uncle could have wheedled Satan himself into forsaking his fire and brimstone.

She flung up one hand at last in surrender. "All right. All right, Uncle. I can hardly withstand both you and Cecily. I suppose I should go tell her at once that I have changed my mind. I only hope she doesn't choke me in her ecstasies."

The old rector nodded in approval, not permitting a sage smile to crease his lips until his niece had gone. He had definitely taken the right tack to persuade Audra, emphasizing Cecily's needs. It wouldn't have done at all for him to admit it was Audra that he was really worried about. He had been observing her solitary habits for some time. The girl was becoming as sequestered as a nun. But if he dared hint that attending that ball would do her more good than Cecily, why Audra would take his head clean off.

CHAPTER 5

By the evening of the ball, if Lady Augusta Penrose had been a female of lesser fortitude, she
would have indulged in a fit of the vapors. A blight
in the hothouse had ruined many of the flowers she
had counted upon for decoration, the extra champagne ordered had failed to arrive, and the French
chef she had imported was engaged in such a dreadful row with the duke's own cook, it was unlikely
that any supper at all would be served that night.
But then, she supposed it was all to be expected
when one was giving a ball in the middle of the
wilderness instead of more civilized London.

These disasters were capped off when she discovered the duke's valet, Bartleby, had given in his
notice . . . again. On the way to make one last harried inspection of the ballroom, Augusta met the
lordly looking manservant stalking down the hall,
his portmanteau in hand.

"Not again, Bartleby," Augusta groaned. "You
have not been quarreling with His Grace tonight of
all nights."

A rather spare individual with the face of a suffering artist, Bartleby drew himself stiffly upright.
"Far be it from me to cause you any distress, m'lady. I am a patient man. I am accustomed to being

sworn at, to say nothing of having a boot shied at me from time to time. But when the master that I have served faithfully all these years, the same one as I have always endeavored to turn out as becomes a gentleman of modest habits, when he accuses me of rigging him out like a *fop* . . . Nay, 'tis too much even for a saint to endure."

"Oh, Bartleby," Augusta cried, but when he made her a smart bow, stalking on his way, she made no effort to stop him. The valet would never get any further than the kitchens where he would permit the housekeeper to offer him tea and a sympathetic ear. And heaven knows, Simon was not the sort of man unable to function without the services of his valet. Still, it was another vexation.

The folds of her silver gauze ball gown rustling, Augusta made her way to the duke's bedchamber door and knocked. Upon her identifying herself, her brother bellowed, "Come in."

Augusta grimaced. She knew Simon would not be enthusiastic about the ball, but if he was going to be in one of his difficult moods, they might as well bar the doors to the castle and be done with it.

She entered to find Simon in his dressing room. He was in his stockinged feet, attired in nothing but a white shirt and black breeches. His expression waxed thunderous as he snapped the starched ends of a stock, preparing to tie his cravat.

"Simon," she demanded, without preamble. "What have you done to poor Bartleby now?"

"That silly ass. I threatened to boil him in his own starch. The dolt kept insisting that in the honor of the occasion, I should allow him to do something special with my cravat arrangement tonight, some damn fool thing he called 'a waterfall.' If I wanted a waterfall about my neck, I'd dump a bucket of water over my head and be done with it."

"Simon!" But Lady Augusta bit back her vexed exclamation, knowing it would not do a particle of good to scold. Besides she had to admit that Simon's taste regarding his attire was impeccable. Having studied the portraits of her ancestors, she might deplore the passage of an age when men garbed themselves in more brilliant colors, rich brocades, cuffs dripping with lace. She often thought that Beau Brummell had done the gentlemen of England no service, persuading them to adopt evening attire that was infinitely more boring. But in Simon's case, the more severe style— the unrelenting black—somehow suited his rugged, dark masculinity.

While Lady Augusta admired her brother's appearance, she saw that he was far from returning the approval. He paused in his exertions with his cravat to scowl at her own gown, his gaze fixed on the plunging neckline.

"Shouldn't you drape yourself with some sort of shawl," he growled. "Or—or stuff a bit of lace there?"

"No. Let me remind you, Simon, I am a married lady, not some chit fresh out of the nursery. Do not attempt to be playing big brother to me tonight. I assure you I am frazzled enough what with everything going wrong."

He turned back to the mirror with a shrug. "All will come right in the end. I have never attended any function of yours that came off less than elegant, Gus. You are ever the perfect hostess."

Although somewhat mollified by the compliment, she said, "I fear the success of this particular function depends more upon its host."

Simon bent closer to the glass, adding another fold to his cravat. "Oh, I'll be so charming, the ladies will be nigh ready to bust their stays with delight." Since this pledge was accompanied by a frown dark enough to shatter the mirror, Augusta did not feel much reassured.

She fidgeted with the things on his dressing table, the silver-handled Sheffield razor, the jars of snuff, the small knife he used for paring his nails, his comb.

Simon felt a twinge of conscience. His placid sister appeared unusually ruffled. Perhaps he could forgo the pleasure of tormenting her, at least for one night.

"I promise you, Gus," he said, "although I may not exactly be the perfect host, I shall endeavor to uphold the honor of the dukes of Raeburn."

"If it is not asking too much, I should also like to see you enjoy yourself a little."

"Ah, that is entirely another matter," Simon said, removing the razor from her grasp before she managed to cut herself. He attempted a taut smile, but could already feel the tension stiffening his neck muscles. Usually he never put himself into such a bother for a mere ball, finding such entertainments a boring nuisance. But this one had somehow attained an importance all out of proportion to the event. He was too much aware that every eye would be trained upon him this eve, all those fond matchmaking mamas, all those coy young maidens tremulous with hope. Simon had been catching enough disturbing bits of gossip during the last fortnight. There was an absurd notion firmly fixed in nearly everyone's mind, that he would award the palm to some eager female this very night.

Simon had never flinched when facing the entire French line, but all this rampant speculation was enough to make him want to bolt.

Seeing Gus so fretful only added to his feeling of being damnably on edge. He barked out an order for her to be still, at least until he had finished dressing. Although she subsided into a striped-silk chair, she kept stealing uneasy glances at him. Uneasy? Nay, more like sheepish.

When he stepped back for one final look, subjecting the severe style of the cravat to his approval, Gus cleared her throat.

"Simon . . . do you recollect that young woman you told me about, the one you found so fascinating?"

"Who the blazes was that?"

"Miss Audra Leigh Masters."

"I wouldn't exactly say that I told you anything about her, Gus. More accurately, you bedeviled the life out of me until I mentioning having met the young woman out——er——walking her dog. But I believe I said no more than that. Certainly nothing about fascination."

"It was rather what you didn't say," Augusta replied. "You didn't call her a hare-brained fool or a die-away ninny. After hearing your opinions of the other ladies hereabouts, I found such reticence positively heartening."

"And so? What about Miss Masters?"

"Nothing," Augusta said airily. "I only thought you might be interested to hear that I found out where she lives."

"I hadn't given it much consideration," he said, reaching for his white satin waistcoat and proceeding to struggle into it. That wasn't precisely a lie. He hadn't thought much about Miss Masters, only caught himself looking for her and the dog, every time he passed by that part of the moat.

Although he was curious, he refused to question his sister as to what she had discovered. He didn't have to. Augusta was determined to tell him.

"Miss Masters happens to be your tenant. She lives at Meadow Lane Lodge."

Meadow Lane. Simon's fingers stilled in the act of buttoning his waistcoat, the mention of that place threatening to bring forth a dangerous flood of memories. The old hunting lodge had been bought up by his father "to prevent rackety young men from coming down from London and scaring our birds." The cottage had been Robert's private retreat, away from the castle. Many times he had entertained Simon there, the pair of them playing truant from the old duke's stern gaze.

"I didn't know the place had been rented," Simon said.

"Did you not instruct Mr. Wylie to do so?"

"I suppose I did." Simon straightened, giving himself a mental shake. He assured himself it would have been sentimental folly to do otherwise, but when he thought of Robert's special place inhabited by a stranger. . . . Sometimes being practical did not come easy.

"So Miss Masters lives there now?" he mused. Practically on his own doorstep. She must keep

82

rather close to the place or surely he would have seen her in the village or come upon her in the lane. But it was not as if he had been deliberately looking for her.

"She lives at Meadow Lane with her younger sister, but no older companion. Rather odd," Augusta said. "But they say she is a considerable heiress."

"Ten thousand pounds a year," Simon mumbled under his breath. His lips twitched as he remembered Audra's indignant speech.

"Her father was the Viscount Sunderly," his sister continued to enlighten him. "Her mother came from good family as well. She was one of the Exeters. Do you recall, Simon? The woman everyone used to call Lady Arabella because she went through husbands at such a rate, no one could ever recall her married name."

"*Her?* The one that now calls herself Countess Monta something?"

"I fear so."

Simon pulled a face. "I met her once when I was traveling through Italy. Good God, the woman is as vulgar and lascivious as Princess Caroline."

"The poor princess. I sometimes think her highness is judged too harshly. They are saying the king will never permit her to be crowned with him."

But the ton gossip held no interest for Simon. He was still digesting the startling information that the absurd, painted female he had met abroad was Miss Masters's mama.

He surprised himself by saying fiercely to his sister, "It makes no odds. Miss Masters is not in the least like Lady Arabella."

"I am pleased to hear it. I shall look forward to

making Miss Masters's acquaintance to—" Augusta clapped her hand over her mouth.

When Simon subjected her to a hard suspicious stare, a guilty flush stole into her cheeks. She rose hastily. "I had best put a few finishing touches onto my own toilette."

"Not so fast, my dear sister." Simon seized her by the elbow. "What d'you mean by that, Gus? Just when do you expect to meet Audra Masters?"

Her smile was a little uncertain, but her eyes danced with mischief. "Why, tonight, of course. I invited her to the ball."

"You what!"

"Don't roar like that, Simon. You hurt my ears."

"Augusta!" His tone became almost as pleading as fierce. "Tell me you didn't. You never sent—"

"I am afraid I did," she said cheerfully. "In quite the grand style, too, I might add. I sent your own secretary Mr. Lawrence to deliver the invitation in your best coach, with footmen in attendance."

Simon emitted a low groan. "So what did she do? Meet poor Lawrence with a loaded blunderbuss?"

"Certainly not, you silly man." Augusta gave a tinkling laugh. "She accepted with the greatest of civility."

Simon was so thunderstruck, he relaxed his grip on Augusta's elbow, permitting her to pull away. With a well-satisfied smile, she made good her escape before Simon could recover his wits enough to bluster. "Blast you, Gus, and your infernal meddling—"

But the door had already closed behind Lady Augusta. In truth, Simon thought grimly, there was little more he could say. He supposed he had furnished Gus with a meddler's license by asking her to arrange this ball in the first place.

But what imp had induced her to invite Audra Masters, and perhaps even more to the point, what had made Miss Masters accept?

"So she wasn't going to come, eh? Not even if I got down on one knee and begged."

As he faced the mirror, a slow, wicked smile spread over his features, but it was nothing compared to the devil's glint in his eyes. This ball that had promised to be such a tedious affair had suddenly taken on an entirely new aspect.

Whistling softly, he finished dressing, taking more pains with his appearance than he ever had in his life.

The Masters's carriage rumbled past the castle gate, moonlight rendering the road a ribbon of silver spiraling toward the great stone keep beyond. The cone-capped towers rose above the line of autumn shorn trees, the stone battlements held spellbound by clouds whispering across the inky sky. It was a night formed for enchantment, adventure, romance. . . .

And Audra wished herself a thousand miles away. As the coach rattled over the ancient drawbridge, she blotted out the chatter of Uncle Matthew and Cecily, her hands clenching tight the nosegay her courtly uncle had presented to her. Why had she allowed Uncle Matt to persuade her into coming? She had wondered that more than once during the past days of preparation, being dragged through silk warehouses, endless fittings with the dressmaker.

And all for what? She detested balls. She was dreadfully awkward at dancing, even more so at the art of making social conversation with strangers. And to add to her discomfort at attending this particular function, *he* would be there.

Raeburn. His Grace of the dark, sardonic eye. The notion of meeting him again made the bodice of her russet-colored gown seemed laced too tight, not allowing enough room for the host of butterflies that had taken up residence beneath her rib cage.

Despising her nervousness, Audra sought to quell it. She'd be hanged if she would permit herself to be intimidated by the mere thought of the man. After all she had cornered the dragon once in his lair, felt the scorch of his fiery breath. She would daresay that she could survive a second encounter.

Besides she kept reminding herself, she was only enduring this misery because of Cecily. And it already seemed worth it to see Muffin looking so deliriously happy. Cecily appeared a veritable princess tonight, all garbed in filmy white from her gown to her satin cloak. A spangled ribbon caught up golden curls framing a face so shining with innocent dreams that most strangely it brought a lump to Audra's throat.

She knew too well that dreams were seldom what they seemed, but she hoped that for just one night, it might prove different for Cecily.

When the coach at last lurched to a halt in the castle courtyard, bewigged grooms sprang forward to open the door. But it was Uncle Matthew who alighted first to offer up his hand to Audra and Cecily. The old man had a most youthful spring to his step tonight. From some ancient trunk, he had unearthed satin knee breeches, a shirt frothy with lace, a brocaded frock coat. But the old-fashioned attire suited him far better than if he had attempted to ape the fashions of the younger men. His excitement at attending the ball seemed not one whit less than Cecily's.

"My ladies," he said, sweeping off his tricorne with a courtly bow that caused his stays to creak.

Cecily giggled as her uncle handed her down. She paused midway upon the coach steps to gape up at the castle. The high arched windows seemed almost iridescent with the glow of myriad lights.

"Oh, Audra," Cecily breathed. "It's all so wonderful. Just as I imagined. There's magic, a certain something in the air tonight—"

"It's called frost," Audra started to mutter, then bit her tongue. No, she had resolved she would say or do nothing to spoil this night for Cecily or her uncle.

"Indeed, it is all most charming," she agreed, giving her starry-eyed sister a gentle prod to get her moving down the steps.

Within the castle hall, liveried footmen hastened forward to take cloaks and hats. This was the newer part of the castle, and although the architecture without had been cleverly designed with the old, Audra noted that the interior could have been part of any Georgian mansion.

When she handed over her own mantle, she felt a tug on the train of her gown. Turning to politely request the gentleman next to her to move his foot, she drew up short, staring into the grinning countenance of Sir Ralph Entwhistle. It had never occurred to Audra that the baronet would be present. She had never known him to do other than tear about the countryside, making some poor horse's life a misery. It was astonishing to see him out of his top boots and buckskins, his stocky frame garbed in tight yellow pantaloons with matching coat. With his wild red hair brushed back, he resembled nothing so much as a squat yellow candle.

"You!" Audra could not helping exclaiming in accents of dismay. "What are you doing here?"

Not in the least taken aback by her bluntness, Sir Ralph chuckled. "I was invited o' course. Thought my sisters may as well have a touch at the duke, too. It'd be a fine thing to have Sophy or Georgy settled here at Raeburn. Good hunting land. Worth the nuisance of attending a ball."

"Indeed?" Audra leveled him a frosty stare. She meant to sweep past him, but the dolt was still standing on the hem of her gown.

"Aw, here now, Miss Masters," he coaxed. "B'gawd woman, you can't still be vexed with me over that little jest I played with Miss Cecily's dog. Why don't you promise me the first dance and we can be friends again?"

"That would be rather difficult since I don't recall our being friends in the first place. Now kindly get off my train."

For a second, she feared Sir Ralph might be too boorish to comply, but he stepped aside at last. However as she stalked away from him, he emitted one of his hee-haw laughs and called after her, "The first dance, Miss Masters!"

Audra longed to tell him if he attempted to stand up with her, his first dance was going to be his last. With difficulty, she checked her temper, recalling her resolve not to cause Cecily any embarras⸱ this evening.

By the time she joined her sister and the Reverend Mr. Masters, taking their place in the receiving line, Audra managed to regain a semblance of calm.

Lit by a massive chandelier, a sweeping marble stair curved upward to the ballroom above. The steps already seemed thronged with silk skirts and fluttering fans waiting to be presented to His Grace.

Audra reflected it was a pity that Raeburn's drawbridge these days was only for ornament, no longer capable of being raised. Of course it had been many centuries since the castle had been attacked, but it was definitely under siege tonight . . . by an army of women.

None of them might be so vulgar as Sir Ralph, admitting that they were also here to have a "touch at the duke." But soft smiles did little to disguise predatory gleams and Raeburn's name was on everyone's lips.

The game was afoot, but the prize tonight was no mere stag or dog fox, but a duke, replete with accompanying lands and titles. Faith, if Raeburn had not shown himself to be so impossibly arrogant, Audra could have felt sorry for the man. But since he had courted this sort of pursuit by giving this silly ball, she did not waste a moment of her sympathy.

As she waited in the reception line, she tried to ignore the fact that her dancing slippers had already begun to pinch her feet. Her heavy chestnut locks done up in a crown of braids seemed to have a dozen hairpins impaled in her scalp. To take her mind from these discomforts, she amused herself by trying to guess which of these women Raeburn might be likely to choose for his duchess. The buxom girl with the shocking decolletage? The icy blonde who was looking down her nose at the rest of the assemblage? Or perhaps that lively little brunette with the voice as shrill as a starling.

As the line inched forward, Audra soon caught a glimpse of Raeburn himself at the head of the stairs. He towered above most of his guests, even the gentlemen, the powerful frame of his square shoulders encased in a black evening coat. The glow of candlelight picked out the flecks of silver in his glossy dark hair did but little to soften the harsh cast of his countenance. Audra sensed he was trying to appear affable as he greeted so many chattering females, but it was difficult. His scowl seemed to come so much more naturally, but perhaps that was all a trick of those heavy black brows.

Still, he looked magnificent, as blazingly fierce as any conqueror of old, very much the duke, the lord of his castle. It suddenly occurred to Audra that she had felt much more on an equal footing when she had just blundered into him out by the moat. He seemed much more formidable looming at the top of the stairs, and her heart gave a flutter of trepidation.

She could have slapped herself for it. After all she wasn't an intruder this time. She was here by his invitation. That reminder did not seem to help, and she started unreasonably when Cecily plucked at her sleeve.

"Audra," Cecily whispered. "Is that the duke?" She indicated an excessively handsome young sprig near the top of the receiving line, his curls as golden as Cecily's own.

"No!" Audra was appalled that her sister could mistake such a stripling for the Duke of Raeburn. "He's right over there, by that petite lady that I suppose must be his sister."

Cecily followed Audra's pointing finger. "Oh," she said, her voice considerably subdued.

Audra was not surprised that her sister should be awed. Though not classically handsome, Raeburn possessed one of those striking countenances no woman could forget. Audra felt obliged to drop a word of warning in Cecily's ear.

"Now, I know you have been weaving a great deal of romantic fantasies in your head, Muffin. But I pray you, don't go losing your heart to the man."

Cecily gave her a very odd look. "N-no, of course not, Audra."

Audra did not have time to say more for at that moment she became aware that a footman was intoning the names of her own party.

"The Reverend Mr. Masters, Miss Audra Masters, and Miss Cecily Holt."

Uncle Matthew made his leg, but he did not waste much time upon the duke, the old rogue moving straightaway to bend over the pretty Lady Augusta's hand. Cecily seemed to have frozen with terror, but at a gentle nudge from Audra, she sank into her curtsy.

Faced with Raeburn's scowl, she only managed to blush and stammer, "Th-thank you for inviting me. You have a very nice castle. I-I have always liked antiquities."

"You are very welcome, young lady," Raeburn said, "but I am not quite that old."

His gruff jest completely discomposed Cecily, and

she all but stumbled in her haste to get away from him. Raeburn rolled his eyes heavenward, and Audra bristled. What more did he expect from the poor child when he had looked as if he were about to have her for breakfast?

Her own nervousness dispelled by anger, Audra determined he would not find her so easily intimidated. When his attention shifted in her direction, she dropped a stiff curtsy.

His eyes skated over her, then started as though in sudden recognition. He then subjected her to a more thorough and, Audra thought, more critical inspection. His gaze locked with hers at last, and her chin came up. She felt like a duelist about to raise her pistol, but she managed to snap out,

"Good evening, Your Grace."

"Miss Masters. I almost did not know you. What have you done to your hair? I liked it better down."

"I did not fix it with any thought of pleasing you."

"Indeed?"

She hadn't offered him her hand, but he took it anyway, engulfing it in the calloused strength of his own. His mouth actually twitched in the semblance of a smile.

He asked, "So have you come here tonight for my head or merely to dance?"

"Neither," she said. "I came to chaperon my sister."

"Sister?" Raeburn's gaze shifted to where Cecily now stood talking to Lady Augusta. Under the older woman's kindness, the girl had recovered and appeared once more aglow with excitement.

"Ah, yes," Raeburn said. "Would that be the same sister who also didn't want to attend the ball?"

Audra refused to rise to this baiting, merely wrenching her hand away. Raeburn bent, making an elaborate show of examining the knees of his breeches. Audra was certain she would be sorry for asking, but she couldn't seem to help herself.

"What, pray, are you doing?"

"Checking for smudge marks." His eyes danced wickedly. "I don't recall getting down on my knees, but I suppose I must have done so. After all, you did say something about being reluctant—"

"I said I would not come if you begged, and I'm beginning to wonder why I did." Audra glared at him. "Did you only invite me here to continue our quarrel?"

"I fear I didn't invite you at all. It was my sister's notion."

Audra felt her face wash red with humiliation. Forgetting all her noble resolves about spoiling her sister's evening, she turned, preparing to gather up Cecily and Uncle Matthew to leave at once.

But Raeburn seized her by the wrist, preventing her. With a soft laugh, he said. "All the same, Miss Masters. I am deuced glad you came."

The look in his eyes was steady, unexpectedly sincere. Audra found it more unnerving than when he mocked her. She said, "I only accepted the invitation, Your Grace, because I believed you would behave like a gentleman."

"No! What did I ever do to give you such a foolish idea as that?"

The thunderstruck expression he feigned coaxed a reluctant smile from her.

"That's better," he approved. "Put up your sword, madam, and I shall do the same. What do you say? Shall we call a truce?"

Audra merely arched both brows. For the second time that evening, she regained possession of her hand from him. Since the next cluster of ladies pressed closer, eager to be presented, he was obliged to let her go.

Simon watched Audra gather up her sister and vanish into the crowded ballroom. It was harder than ever to return to his task of greeting these other insipid females, but he managed. Seeing Miss Masters had given his spirits an odd lift, rendering him almost gracious.

He had nearly given up on her arrival, thinking she must have changed her mind. Since he scarce heeded the names flung at him, he had not been aware of her presence until he had glanced around to find her standing before him.

Even then he hadn't recognized her at first. She looked so different in that rather drab brown gown, her hair done up so primly in those braids. He had been disappointed, wondering if memory had failed him, if he had been incorrect in fancying her something out of the common way.

But one look into those forthright eyes had reassured him. He should be ashamed of himself for how he had teased her, deliberately provoking her. But her eyes turned the most delightful storm gray when she was angry, like a warrior queen dispensing her thunderbolts.

Simon never thought he would look forward to such a thing as the first dance, but he became impatient for the orchestra to strike up the music.

He was down to the last few guests straggling in when his sister stole a chance to whisper to him. Lady Augusta's smooth brow was marred by a frown.

"I must say, Simon. Your Miss Masters was certainly a pretty little thing with engaging manners, but I scarce expected such an infant to capture your attention."

"You got the sisters mixed up, m'dear," Simon murmured back. "Miss Masters was the other one."

"The tall one with the flashing eyes who looked like she wanted to poleax you." Augusta brightened at once. "But, Simon, how delightful."

Simon gave his sister a wry glance. "Just don't be handing her any weapons."

He made a smart bow to the last late arrival, then excused himself. As he stalked eagerly across the ballroom, the crowd parted and fell back for him.

A hush seemed to fall all over the room and, at any other time, Simon would have found the air of breathless expectation embarrassing. Every lady present craned her neck, waiting to see whom he would favor with the first dance.

But they were as doomed to disappointment as himself. The strains of the first cotillion struck up, but in a room full of eager females, Simon could not locate the one lady he sought.

Miss Masters appeared to have vanished.

CHAPTER 6

Audra never had any intention of trying to hide when she first entered the ballroom. Having survived the ordeal of seeing Raeburn again, she had merely meant to blend in with the elegant frieze adorning the walls.

She felt that she could in good conscience do so, having done her duty by Cecily, seeing the girl suitably partnered. Unlike many of the other more coy maidens waiting to see whom the duke would choose, Cecily had been glad to award the first dance to the poetic Mr. Gilmore.

"Though I know he can be a bit silly," she had confessed to Audra. "I would far rather stand up with him even if the duke should ask me. I fear I would find dancing with His Grace most terrifying."

Audra could scarce blame her sister after the way Raeburn had overwhelmed Cecily with his fierce scowl when she had made him her curtsy. Yet Audra had to admit the man could be unexpectedly charming after his own gruff fashion. She could not help recalling that brief moment he had looked straight into her eyes, remarking that he was "deuced glad she'd come."

The memory had a strange effect on her, bringing a rush of warmth to her cheeks that she fought to quell. She still concurred with Cecily's view that it would be remarkably uncomfortable to have to dance with Raeburn. Any lady foolish enough to do so tonight would be a marked woman, the focus of much critical staring and speculation. Cecily had been quite wise to prefer the more bland, but less notorious attentions of a Mr. Gilmore.

As for Audra, she had no intention of dancing with anyone, despite how her Uncle Matthew scolded. When Cecily moved off to take her position in the first quadrille, Audra took up hers beneath the shadow of one of the room's towering pillars.

Uncle Matthew followed, frowning. " 'Tis not necessary for you to linger there, m'dear. Those pillars have been holding up the roof for a long time without any assistance from you."

"You are quite right, Uncle. As soon as the dancing begins, I mean to find a chair."

"What! Be seated among the quizzes and dowagers. I won't hear of it, Audra—"

"Now, Uncle, I warned you before we came that I meant to do no dancing, not even with you. So I suggest you seek out some other lady to bedevil. There will be many needing your gallant consolation once the duke makes his selection."

Although the old rector pursed his lips with disappointment, he did as she asked. She could hear him grumbling as he moved away and kept a wary eye upon him. She was still not certain the old man would not return with some sprig in tow, attempting to partner her off. But as she watched her uncle's retreat, Audra realized she stood in far more immediate danger.

Pressing past a plump turbaned dowager, Audra

saw Sir Ralph Entwhistle heading in her direction, his bright red hair a beacon even in the crowded ballroom. The vacuous smile on his face and the determined set to his chin left Audra in no doubt of his intentions.

The fool thought he was coming to claim his dance. Audra tensed. Was there any way of discouraging a man so completely dense? Audra could think of but one. Unfortunately, drawing Sir Ralph's cork would just attract the sort of attention she most deplored.

Only one other alternative remained to her, and that was flight. Frantically she glanced around for a suitable retreat. Spotting what she thought was a curtained alcove, Audra headed for it.

Behind her, she heard Sir Ralph's baffled cry. "Miss Masters." As persistent as one of his own hounds, he kept coming. Audra quickened her steps. Darting beneath the curtain, she discovered that the arch led not to an alcove but a long corridor.

She'd never make it to the other end before Sir Ralph spotted her. Instead she raced to the first door she saw, opened it, and hurled herself inside. Leaning up against the oak portal, she attempted to still her breath, putting her ear against the wood to listen.

Presently she heard the tread of heavy footsteps and Sir Ralph calling, "Halloa! Miss Masters?" He sounded so very like a mournful dog, baying because he had lost the scent, that Audra had to stifle a gasp of laughter.

She waited, scarce daring to breathe until she heard his footsteps recede. Flooded with relief, she still did not stir, determined not to make her way back to the ballroom until she was certain Sir Ralph would have had enough time to inflict himself upon some other unfortunate female.

Shifting slightly, she glanced about her, for the first time taking stock of the place in which she had sought refuge. Light from the fire left blazing upon the hearth cast flickering shadows up the walls, walls lined from floor to ceiling with shelves of books.

Audra stood transfixed, pressing her hands to her heart. She had heard tales of the magnificent library to be found at Castle Raeburn, but never in her wildest imaginings had she ever fancied a treasure trove such as this.

Shivering with delight, she stepped away from the door. Locating a branch of candles, she lit the wicks, then like a pilgrim approaching a shrine, she paced reverently along the stacks, breathing in the heady scent of leather, caressing the embossed lettering on the spines.

Any number of intriguing titles leaped out at her, causing her head to spin. Chaucer and Milton nestled side by side with Fielding and Shakespeare. Among some of the newer-looking books she found Byron.

With a tiny sigh, she pulled a volume of *Ivanhoe* from the shelf. What with all the hubbub over this blasted ball, she still had been unable to finish the book. Wistfully, she thumbed to the page where she had been obliged to leave off on far too many occasions. As she fingered the book, she became aware that an armchair stood just at her elbow, its overstuffed cushions looking far too inviting.

She half started to sink into it and stopped,

horrified at herself. No, truly, she couldn't. Even now she could hear distant strains of music coming from the ballroom, reminding her where she ought to be.

But by now Cecily must be moving through the steps of the quadrille with Mr. Gilmore. Likely Uncle Matthew was also agreeably engaged. Who would miss Audra if she were to take a few minutes, just long enough to finish the end of one chapter?

Perching gingerly on the edge of the chair, Audra was tempted to ease off her shoes for a moment. The slippers had begun to pinch abominably, but she feared that once removed, she might never get the wretched things back on. As she perused a few lines of the book, she soon forgot her aching feet. Becoming ever more absorbed, she settled deeper against the cushions. After a time the muted sounds of music and laughter coming from the ballroom faded. She scarce heard the mantel clock chiming out the passing of the hour.

Torquilstone Castle was in flames. The villain, Bois-Guilbert, managed to seize Rebecca as he made his escape and Audra rode with them, flinching at every arrow that whizzed past her.

Caught up in the tale, Audra did not notice the library door swinging open until it was too late. It slammed to, alarming her so that she nigh jumped from her chair.

For one dreadful moment, she feared it might be Sir Ralph come looking for her or, at the least, some lofty butler who would demand to know what she was doing in here. As she peered round from her chair, she wished she could shrink to the size of inkprint and vanish into the book.

Worse than any supercilious servant, it was Raeburn.

Oblivious to her presence, he strode in, looking like a harried fox gone to ground. With grim purpose, he moved to a cabinet against the opposite wall and drew forth a brandy decanter. As he sloshed some of the liquid into a glass, Audra froze, unable to move a muscle, which was quite absurd. As soon as Raeburn whipped about, he was bound to see her, no matter how still she sat.

She was correct for as he shifted, preparing to toss down the brandy, he paused with the glass halfway to his lips, staring at her. His brows rose in astonishment.

"Miss Masters," he said. He set the glass down with a sharp click. "I wondered where the deuce you were hiding."

"I-I wasn't hiding." Audra flushed, annoyed with herself for stammering and even more so for the guilty impulse to whip the book behind her like a naughty child caught pilfering sweetmeats.

But as Raeburn's gaze tracked from her discomfited face to the book she clutched, he looked more amused than vexed. "You do seem to have a habit of making yourself quite at home upon my estate, madam."

Audra shot to her feet. "I beg your pardon. If I had any notion *you* would come in here—"

"I know. You would have fled to the Antipodes. Oh, do sit down, Miss Masters. We called a truce, remember?"

When she didn't comply, he barked, "Sit down."

Though disgusted by her own meekness, Audra obeyed him. Not that she minded being bellowed at, but Raeburn seemed exactly the sort of man to back up his commands with force if necessary. Besides, she was not about to let His Grace think she could be so easily frightened away. She settled back in the chair, resting the book on her lap with forced casualness.

"I didn't mean to intrude," she said. " 'Tis only I have never seen anything like your library. And the fire had been left burning in here. It was all so inviting."

"The fire is always left kindled for me. I spend a great deal of my time here, though I always doubted the place would hold much interest for my guests, especially the ladies."

"Perhaps it wouldn't for most. I always seem to be different."

"So you are, very different." Raeburn was not the only person to tell her so, but he was the first person to sound so approving. She felt more strangely flustered than if he had paid her a lavish compliment.

When he stalked toward her, her heart gave a disconcerting thud, although all he did was pluck the book from her hands, glance at the title, then return it to her.

"*Ivanhoe.* I've had no opportunity to examine that one myself. Is there any merit to it?"

"I can scarce say. I have been interrupted too many times. But it was wrong of me to be reading when I should be in the ballroom."

"Why? I am sure you are feeling no more eager to return to that tedious affair than I am."

"Tedious? But if you feel that way . . ." She trailed off, knowing it was none of her concern, but she couldn't refrain from asking, "Why the deuce did you ever have the blasted thing?"

"Be hanged if I know." He grimaced. "It seemed like a good idea at the time. I fear that as a duke, I am not blessed with your freedom and independence. I have certain obligations, even though I, too, am a bachelor and fiercely proud of it."

"Yes, I had forgotten. Your legendary search for a bride." Audra could not prevent a smile escaping.

"Do you find it that amusing? I admit I have a face and temper like the devil, but I can surely find some wench who will have me."

"Likely too many of them. I only smiled because it all seems so silly—Er, that is, I mean . . ." Audra floundered, trying to recover from her want of tact, but Raeburn would have none of it.

"Come, Miss Masters. You have never hesitated to insult me before. Why turn shy now?"

Very well. He had asked for it. She crossed her arms, her voice laced with scorn. "Did you really believe you were going to find a wife tonight in that ballroom? That all it would take was one look, one glance, and you would immediately know which lady to choose? Forgive me, but you scarce seem the sort to be prone to such romantic nonsense."

"I am not, any more than you are. The idea that one would come across one special person that one would find so intriguing . . . Well, of course, it is absurd. And yet . . ." His eyes locked with hers. "And yet," he added softly. "One must begin somewhere."

"I suppose one must," Audra replied, surprised to hear her own voice sound so breathless. She had never realized it before, but it could be rather dangerous to stare too long into any man's eyes, especially eyes possessed of such fierce, dark passion as Raeburn's. She felt oddly lightheaded and was quick to lower her gaze.

"It will scarce aid Your Grace in your search to linger here. You should get back to the ballroom. After all, you are the host."

"Justly rebuked, Miss Masters." He held out his hand to her. "Very well. Come on then."

Audra only stared in dismay at those long, tanned fingers, their latent strength quite evident. "Oh, n-no. I had rather hoped you might permit me to remain—"

"The devil I will. I fear I am not that generous, madam." He took the book from her and dropped it on the side table. Seizing her by the hand, he tugged her to her feet. "If I must suffer through this cursed ball, so must you."

Audra opened her lips to protest, but what could she say? After all, it was his castle. She permitted him to lead her from the library with great reluctance. But as they started down the hallway, she did complain.

"There is no need to keep such a grip upon my arm, sir. It is not as if I were planning to run away."

"Truly? It seems to me you have a very bad habit of doing so, Miss Masters. I wouldn't want to lose you again. I believe we will be just in time to take our places in the next set forming."

"You may do so, but I am not engaged to stand up with anyone."

"I didn't think you were or you could hardly be going to dance with me."

"What!" Audra came to an abrupt halt beneath the arch that led back into the ballroom, her dismay only second to her astonishment. Dance with *her?*

Was His Grace often given to these mad starts?

"You cannot mean, that . . . that is I am honored, but I don't dance, Your Grace."

"Neither do I," the duke said pleasantly. "So this should prove a most interesting exercise."

Maintaining a firm grip upon her arm, he propelled her inexorably forward. Audra could already sense the eyes fixing in her direction, heads nodding together, the whispers behind fans. She sought to quell a hot blush.

"Your Grace, I fear I have not made myself clear. I don't want to dance."

But with his customary high-handedness, he led her to the head of the set. Too proud to plead with him, to confess her own clumsiness or even how sore her feet already were, Audra held her head up high. When he finally released her arm, she could do naught but remain. To flee from his side would only cause the whispers to increase.

As the music began, Raeburn swept her a bow full of mocking challenge. Audra sank into a furious curtsy, hissing between her teeth. "You are going to be very sorry for this, Your Grace."

His lips twitched in infuriating fashion. He was still smiling when they came together in the movement of the dance. Audra smiled sweetly back at him, then stomped on his foot. His smirk vanished in an astonished gasp. "You vixen! You did that a-purpose."

As they separated, Audra skirted round him, managing to deliver a swift kick to his shin.

Raeburn choked back an oath, his brows crashing together. "I'm warning you, madam . . ." But the rest of his threat was lost as the steps of the dance took them apart.

When they next came back together, she caught him square on the ankle.

"Damnation!" Raeburn growled. His black scowl would have daunted anyone else, but Audra was far too caught up in her own anger. In fact, she could never recall taking such a militant pleasure in any dance. She paraded down the line, planning her next assault.

Approaching Raeburn again, she prepared to aim for his instep. But his eyes narrowed, Raeburn struck first, treading upon her toes. Audra stifled a yelp. Simmering with indignation, she readied for the next skirmish, a sharp kick that caused him to falter.

His thunderous expression boded ill for her, and Audra almost knew a craven impulse to retreat. But there was no help for it. The perfidious patterns of the dance brought her back to his side where he tromped upon her other foot.

Audra bit her lip to keep from swearing. Her poor toes, already pinched tight by the slippers, were in no condition to tolerate more of Raeburn's abuse. Much as she hated being the first to cry enough, she became uncomfortably aware of the shocked stares of the other dancers in their set.

When next she came face-to-face with Raeburn, she curbed her temper, settling for a glower rather than a blow.

"You, sir, are no gentleman," she snapped.

"And you, madam, are assuredly no lady."

After which exchange of insults, they finished out the dance in grim silence, more after the manner of a pair of duelists, circling each other with wary respect.

As soon as the last notes of the dance sounded,

Audra made the briefest of curtsies, preparing to stalk away as fast as her throbbing feet would let her. But Raeburn linked his arm roughly through hers.

"It is my habit, madam, to escort my partner from the floor, no matter how ill-used I have been."

Audra longed to shake him off, but she supposed she had already created enough of a scene for one evening. Clenching her teeth, she permitted Raeburn to lead her to the side of the ballroom.

"If you feel ill-used, it was entirely your own doing," she said. "I told you I didn't want to stand up with you. I can make enough of a spectacle of myself without your assistance."

"I don't doubt it, especially if you treat an offer to dance as if a man had offered you an insult."

"Offer! More like demand. And it was an insult. You only did it to torment me."

"Can you imagine no other reason?"

"No!"

Having guided her to the side of the ballroom, he subjected her to a hard stare. "It might have occurred to you that . . . Never mind." His jaw tightened. "Your servant, madam."

Sweeping her a curt bow, he stalked away. Still seething, Audra watched him go, but her anger was tempered by the uncomfortable feeling that she had somehow wronged him. Even if he had forced her to dance, she had behaved in an abominably unladylike fashion, even for the eccentric Miss Audra Leigh Masters. Perhaps she even owed the duke an apology. But at least, he would have the good sense never to demand that she dance with him again.

That thought, however, did not offer her the satisfaction that it should have. Rather it only seemed to add to her misery, especially when the strains of a waltz filled the room and she observed Raeburn leading another lady onto the floor.

She was a dark-haired beauty, willowy, graceful, a diamond of the first water. But the way the creature simpered, looking up at Raeburn with such toad-eating deference, was enough to turn Audra's stomach. Unable to endure watching anymore, Audra limped off to find an obscure corner of the room.

Locating a small gilt settee half-hidden by a spray of flowers, Audra sank down upon the cushion. She never carried anything so frippery as a fan, but for once she wished she had one of the blasted things. The room seemed unbearably warm, but whether from her recent exercise or her bout of temper, Audra could not have said.

Bending over to massage the toe of her slipper, realizing she had the devil of a blister forming, Audra would have been content to pass the rest of the evening in quiet obscurity. But she had completely forgotten her initial reason for escaping to the library—that is until Sir Ralph suddenly loomed above her to remind her.

The baronet looked for all the world like a sulky red-haired troll. "B'gawd, Miss Masters," he accused. "You forgot our dance."

Audra thought if she heard the word "dance" upon a man's lips one more time tonight, she would have a fit of apoplexy. Stretching out one slipper, wriggling her sore foot, she said, "You must hold me excused, sir. I fear I will be doing no more dancing tonight."

"I shouldn't wonder. I watched you dancing with Raeburn." Sir Ralph brayed a laugh. "The squire and I got up a wager of which you would be the first to lame the other."

"Wonderful," Audra muttered. "I am pleased to have provided you with such diversion, sir."

She winced when Sir Ralph plunked himself beside her with such force the entire settee seemed to tremble. "Well, it doesn't matter a ha'penny about the dance. I'd far rather sit and talk."

Audra nearly groaned aloud, wishing she had claimed sore ears instead of feet. At any other time, she could have dealt with Sir Ralph, but she was feeling far too wearied from her quarrel with Raeburn. Naturally the baronet's conversation settled upon one thing: his fox hunting.

Audra thought of telling him once and for all that she found his notion of sport cruel and disgusting, but she knew it would be a waste of breath. The fool would never comprehend her feelings. So she listened in dour silence while Entwhistle lamented the dearth of foxes.

"Not many new cubs. It's going to be a bad year," Sir Ralph said. "Which is why you must no longer ever speak to Mr. Cecil. He's a vulpicide."

"A *vulpicide*?"

"He shot a vixen raiding his henhouse."

"But you kill foxes all the time," Audra protested indignantly.

"That's different. I do it proper, hunting them with hounds. Cornered a feisty cub just the other morning, but some of my young dogs aren't so well trained. B'gawd, Ratterer and Bellman tore that fox to shreds before I could even claim the pads and mask."

When Entwhistle went on to describe the scene in more vivid detail, Audra felt herself go pale. By the time he reached the part about what remained of the cub's blood-soaked brush, Audra truly thought she was going to be ill.

Rescue came from an unexpected quarter, an acid voice interrupting Sir Ralph's boisterous flow of words.

"I don't believe Miss Masters cares for your hunt stories, Entwhistle."

Both Audra and the baronet glanced round to discover the Duke of Raeburn leaning up against the back of the settee. How long he had stood there listening, Audra had no idea. She despised herself for the way her heart leaped, how foolishly glad she felt to see him.

As for Sir Ralph, although he rose respectfully to his feet, he thrust out his lower lip. "Pish, Miss Masters takes a keen interest in the sport, which is more than can be said for some, Your Grace. What's this foul rumor I've been hearing tonight that you may start forbidding my hunt to cross your land?"

" 'Tis no rumor, but a fact, sir," Raeburn said levelly. "Besides the fact you ruin my tenant's crops, I heard young Worthington near snapped his neck jumping one of my hedges the other day. If anyone is carted off on a hurdle, it's not going to be on my estate."

"Damme!" Sir Ralph roared. "B'gawd, I've never heard such an attitude. 'Tis positively un-English." When Raeburn stiffened, the baronet managed to lower his voice, assuming a more placating tone. "Not that I don't understand. Your brother's unfortunate accident and all. But a man can cut his stick a hundred other ways than hunting, and it happened so many years ago."

Audra thought she detected a flash of pain in

Raeburn's eyes, quickly shuttered away. But all he said was, "I believe you are keeping my sister waiting, Entwhistle. She is expecting to dance with you."

Though clearly prepared to argue the hunt question all night, Raeburn's words took Sir Ralph aback.

"The Lady Augusta?" The baronet's eyes rounded. "Is she, then? B'gawd, I wouldn't want to offend my hostess." And looking immensely flattered, Sir Ralph bustled off.

Audra angled a reproachful glance at the duke. "What an unhandsome thing to have done to your sister."

"Wasn't it, though?" Raeburn's grim expression relaxed into the barest hint of a smile. "It scarce signifies, for if I know Gus, she has already promised every dance by now."

The mischief in those dark eyes almost invited her to smile back at him. Just barely Audra recollected that she and Raeburn were supposed to be at odds with each other.

He folded his arms, staring down at her. "Well, aren't you even going to thank me?"

"For what?"

"Rescuing you from the company of that redheaded oaf."

"I am quite capable of dealing with Sir Ralph myself." Audra started to stand, preparing to stalk away. But her foot twisted just enough to rub the slipper against her blister. She sank back down, sucking in her breath between her teeth.

"What the deuce is amiss?" Raeburn asked. "Are you hurt?"

"No, 'tis nothing. Only my blasted foot."

He settled beside her on the settee, his brow furrowing with concern. "I'm sorry. It is all my fault for being so cursed rough. Do you have a sprain or only a bruise?"

Audra shrank away, whisking her slippers further beneath the hem of her gown. "There is no need for you to be so concerned. My injury is none of your doing. It is only these dratted shoes. They have been paining me all evening. They are about two sizes too small."

"Of all the confounded folly. Why the blazes didn't you have them made to fit?"

"Because." Audra's cheeks stung with mortified pride. She blurted out, "Because it is bad enough being so tall, without having my feet seem so large as well."

There! Now that she had made confession of this one small but foolish vanity, perhaps he would leave her in peace. Though he looked a little astonished, he said gruffly, "There's no disgrace in being tall, and I prefer women to have large feet rather than mince about."

"You are utterly ridiculous, sir." But a laugh escaped Audra in spite of herself.

Raeburn nodded with approval. "I wondered if I would ever be able to persuade you to smile at me again."

Audra tried to resume her pokerlike expression, but it was hopeless, especially when Raeburn continued, "Whether your afflicted foot is my fault or not, I suppose I do owe you an apology for what I did earlier, forcing you to dance. My sister, Gus, will tell you I do have a tendency to be a bit of a bully."

"Pray don't apologize, at least not for tramping

my toes. I fear I asked for that. As my sister would tell you, I have an infernally bad temper."

"You were right to be angry. I was being selfish, consulting only my own feelings and not yours. Contrary to what you might believe, Miss Masters, I didn't ask you to dance with me just to enrage you. I did so because I wanted to stand up with you more than any other lady present."

"Oh," was all Audra could think of to say. Her reply seemed foolishly inadequate even to her. "I can't imagine why Your Grace would—I am sure there are many more charming women present."

"Aye, I have near been charmed to death tonight. I've never been so flattered, so fawned over. 'Yes, Your Grace. No, Your Grace. The sun is blue if you say so, Your Grace.' I swear the lot of these females would court the devil himself, if the title of duchess came with it."

"Poor man! I could kick you again if it would make you feel better." But although she sought to mask a sudden bout of shyness beneath her flippant tone, Audra did not want him to think her wholly unsympathetic. "I do understand," she said. "I was pestered nigh to madness with unwanted suitors my first Season. All because of my fortune, you know."

"Ten thousand pounds a year," Raeburn agreed with a quizzing smile.

Although she blushed to be reminded of her vulgar boast, Audra continued, "But since there was no reason I had to be married, I eventually managed to drive everyone away."

"Rather like the princess in that old story, living in her castle behind her wall of thorns."

"Yes, if you like. Only I would never be caught

napping. If there were any prince fool enough to scale my wall, I would greet him with an unsheathed sword."

"Would you? I give you fair warning, Miss Masters. I am a fair hand with a blade."

Audra started, scarce knowing how to interpret such a remark. If it had been anybody else but Raeburn, she almost might have supposed him to be flirting with her. A little daunted, she suddenly realized how close he sat. Of course the settee was rather small.

Sitting rigidly upright, she gave a nervous cough to clear her throat. "This is getting to be a very silly conversation. Perhaps we had best talk of something else. Why don't you tell me about your travels abroad?" she suggested desperately.

"My dear Miss Masters, you are a glutton for punishment. Hasn't this ball provided you with boredom enough?"

"No, truly, I would not find it boring at all. That is one of the drawbacks to being a spinster," she said wistfully. "One can never go anywhere, unless one drags along some dreadful companion. Certainly not anywhere exciting like Greece ... or Rome."

"But surely you could visit Italy anytime you chose. Doesn't your mother live—" Raeburn broke off, looking mighty uncomfortable as Audra found gentlemen often did when mentioning Lady Arabella.

"Y-you know my mother?" she faltered.

"Well, er ... yes, I did meet her just once during the course of my travels." It was an innocuous enough statement, but it was what His Grace was not saying that seemed to speak volumes.

Audra knew she should just let it rest there, but she couldn't seem to do so. She attempted a smile that was more a pain-filled grimace. "Such a small world, isn't it? My mother is so high-spirited. I-I suppose she flirted with you most shockingly."

"Of course not," Raeburn said almost too quickly. "Only look at my face, Miss Masters. Do I appear the sort of man a woman would want to flirt with?"

Audra did scan his features most intently, from that hawklike nose to the harsh lines carved by his mouth, to the lowering dark brows that could not quite disguise the kindness in his eyes as he lied to spare her feelings. Yes, Audra was disconcerted to discover, he was exactly the sort of man she would wish to flirt with if she were at all adept at the art.

That realization was almost as embarrassing as her suspicion that likely her own mother had cast out lures to the duke. When he tried to lighten her mood by launching into an anecdote of how he had once nigh fallen into the canal in Venice, she stopped him.

"I am afraid I have kept Your Grace here talking long enough. You should be paying more heed to your other guests. Dancing or some such."

Raeburn's dark look showed exactly what he thought of her suggestion, so she hastened to add, "All these determined ladies might wax dangerous if deprived of your company for too long. I daresay your absence has already been remarked."

Raeburn did glance about him as if half expecting to find some predatory female ready to spring at him from the floral arrangement. Though he scowled, he rose to his feet, the gesture rife with resignation.

"Very well. I shall go do my cursed duty, but only under one condition."

Audra regarded him warily. "Which is?"

"You will let me take you into supper later."

Caught somewhere between delight and dismay, Audra stammered. "Oh, n-no, I couldn't."

"Why not? All right, so you don't dance. But even you, my redoubtable Miss Masters, must eat."

"Of course, I do," she said with a reluctant laugh. "But—"

Her protest was silenced when he captured one of her hands. "As my one true friend, Miss Masters, after flinging me to these ravening hordes of women, you should at least promise me some respite."

His words might be light, teasing, but his gaze was intent. Audra sighed. Was there ever any other man who knew how to use his eyes to such advantage?

"All right. I shall sit with you at supper."

He smiled, carrying her hand to his lips. Then, as if he feared she might yet change her mind, he bowed and was gone.

Audra sat perfectly still for long seconds after the duke vanished, staring at her hand as if she had never seen it before. Raeburn's kiss had not been in the least romantic, but rather brusque. Yet her skin still tingled from the rough brush of his lips. She drew in a tremulous breath, feeling more strange than she ever had in her life, as if she wanted to laugh and cry all at the same time. She, who had never been given to any excess of emotion.

She told herself she should have remained firm, refused Raeburn's demand to take her into supper. But he had called her his "one true friend." Was there any higher compliment a man could pay to a woman? Audra liked the sound of it as a thought suddenly occurred to her. Given her reclusive lifestyle, she had never had many friends.

Glancing up toward the window panes, blackened by night, the ball suddenly seemed more interminable than ever, but for a different reason. With an almost feverish impatience, she tried to calculate how much time remained until midnight, the hour supper would be served.

It would seem longer if she just sat here, ticking off the minutes. She supposed she ought to go look out for Cecily, especially considering she had not seen her sister for some time. A very poor chaperon she was turning out to be. Standing up, she emerged from her hiding place, preparing to skirt cross the center of a ballroom where another lively waltz was taking place.

Odd that she had never noticed, but there was something rather delightful about a ball, the whirl of colors, the graceful way the dancers dipped and swirled. Her feet were feeling a little better, and she was almost sorry she had sent Raeburn in quest of another partner.

As she made her way past the column of pillars, she caught herself humming with the music. She saw Raeburn in the midst of the dancers and had to choke back a laugh. He had a rare and charming smile upon his face as he waltzed with a sweet-faced elderly dame who looked old enough to be his grandmama. Audra could only begin to imagine what must be the indignation of all the young ladies present. What a teasing devil he was.

But Audra's amusement was tempered by the fact that nowhere amid all the circling couples did she spy Cecily. Granted the ladies outnumbered the men tonight, but Audra had never expected that her lovely sister would have to sit out a dance.

Imagining what Cecily's chagrin must be, Audra hastened to find her. Most of the partnerless ladies were clustered in disconsolate groups to one side of the ballroom. As Audra made her way toward them, she squeezed behind several gilt-trimmed chairs where some of the women had taken refuge.

She overheard the dark-haired beauty whom Raeburn had danced with earlier complaining in peevish accents to a formidable dowager in a purple turban.

"We may as well go home, Mama. Since the duke has stopped dancing with any of the eligible ladies, it is obvious he has settled upon his choice."

"What utter nonsense, Charlene. Whom do you think he has chosen?"

"That tall, plain creature, the one who stepped all over him during the cotillion. His Grace was over there in that corner, talking to her forever. Alicia Wright even saw him kiss her hand."

"That Masters woman? The eccentric spinster who lives like a hermit. Ridiculous! Good lord, I have heard that she is even *bookish.*"

Audra knew she should not listen to any more of this, but she suddenly felt rooted to the spot with dismay, unable to move.

Another older woman whom Audra vaguely recognized as Mrs. Wright, the mother of six unwed daughters, leaned forward to join in the conversation. "Eccentric Miss Masters may be, but also possessed of a large fortune, according to Lady Coleby."

The turbaned one sniffed. "Sophia Coleby is a

wicked gossip, but she does usually know everything. But surely the duke need not take fortune into account in his choice of a bride."

"My dear," Mrs. Wright sneered. "The gentlemen always take that into account."

No! It was all Audra could do not to break in upon the women and protest. Raeburn wasn't counting upon any such thing, because he had not chosen Audra for anything other than a friend. It was horrid of these old tabbies to be implying otherwise.

But worse was to follow. Mrs. Wright lowered her voice, but remained disastrously audible. "Of course you know whose daughter Miss Masters is. That vulgar creature known in London circles simply as Lady Arabella. Widowed four times and married again to say nothing of . . ."

Behind the cover of her fan, Mrs. Wright whispered something to the turbaned dowager which caused that lady to stiffen with shock.

"Well," she huffed. "That explains why Miss Masters is so shameless in setting her cap at the duke. Like mother, like daughter, I always say."

Mrs. Wright gave a sour laugh. "I fear Miss Masters will never be able to rival Lady Arabella in the number of marriages. The poor dear is getting such a late start, and the duke is a remarkably healthy specimen." Mrs. Wright stood up, shaking out her skirts. "I grow stiff from just sitting here. Shall we take a turn about the room?"

"We might as well." The purple turban also rose. "Come along, Charlene. Perhaps if you keep moving, your want of a partner will not be as noticeable."

The two dowagers rustled off, the pouting dark beauty trailing in their wake. Audra stepped slowly forward, then leaned on the back of one of the vacated chairs for support. She touched a hand to her cheek, astonished to find it was possible to blanch and still burn at the same time.

If things had been arranged more fairly, it would be possible for her to stalk after those creatures, slap Mrs. Wright with her glove for bandying Audra's name about, challenge her to a duel. But the world only favored gentlemen with such an outlet. A lady was ever obliged to smile, confining her barbs to her tongue, and the heavens help those possessing no claws to defend themselves.

Audra knew she shouldn't pay any heed to malicious gossip. She flattered herself that she was usually tougher than that. But Mrs. Wright's remarks were not all easily dismissed. To have herself compared to Lady Arabella, to be said to be like her mama! God save her, that was one raking of claws that had drawn blood.

And yet she had to absolve even those two harpies. No, the fault was her own, entirely hers. She had known any woman Raeburn bestowed attention upon tonight would attract undue attention, jealous criticism. At what point had she allowed herself to forget that—when he had smiled too deep into her eyes, when he had teased her into forgetting her shame about Mama's behavior, when he had kissed her hand?

It scarce mattered when she had become a fool, only that she had. Most heartily did she now regret her promise to Raeburn that he could take her to supper. She might possess neither beauty nor charm, but one thing she did have was pride.

Supping with the duke would really set tongues

to wagging. But far worse than any gossip was the doubts that had been sown in Audra's mind.

Was she so sure herself that Raeburn's only design in courting her was friendship? The kiss to her hand, forcing her to dance, repeatedly seeking her out, could those have any other significance? She couldn't bring herself to think of Raeburn as a fortune hunter, or even that he would consider marrying her for any reason.

It was all so absurd, so confusing. Only one thing was certain. The prospect of facing him again filled her with a sensation of panic. If there was only some way she could vanish before midnight, be far away from here. Yet Cecily would never forgive Audra for tearing her away from the ball that early.

She was still pondering what to say to the girl when she finally located her sister. Or rather Cecily found her first, fairly hurling herself into Audra's arms. Before Audra could speak a word, she was dumbfounded to hear Cecily's declaration.

"Oh, Audra, I want to go home."

Audra blinked, attempting to recover from her astonishment. But instead of relief that her own escape should be made so easy, Audra felt alarmed. Cecily was quite pale, with a glazed look in her eyes.

"Muffin, what's wrong? Have you not been having a good time either?"

"I have been having a wonderful time." A large tear escaped to trickle off the end of Cecily's pert nose. "B-but now I feel like I am going to be s-sick."

She clutched a hand to her stomach, her face going from white to hintings of green.

Audra slipped her arm about Cecily's waist.

"Don't cry, love. I will take you home at once. Where is Uncle Matt?"

"In the card room, I th-think."

"Well, there is no need to disturb him. We can send the coach back to fetch him later. Come on."

Bracing Cecily, she led the girl toward the main door of the ballroom. Although her concern for Cecily was quite real, Audra experienced a sense of shame as well. Her solicitude was perhaps a shade too eager, as if she exploited Cecily's illness to cover her own cowardly desire to flee.

Guiding Cecily down the long, curving stair back to the lower hall, Audra despatched a footman to send for her coach and fetch their cloaks.

Cecily sagged against Audra, a picture of misery. "Shouldn't we take our leave of Lady Augusta and the duke?" she asked.

"No!" Audra lowered her voice, managing to add in a calmer tone. "We will send round our excuses later. You don't want to be sick here all over His Grace's marble tiles, do you?"

"Oh, n-no, Audra." She stood, listlessly docile while Audra swept her cloak about her shoulders. Audra pulled up the hood, hiding drooping blond curls, a face most woebegone. Audra tried to be gentle, hoping her own nervousness was not apparent. Her chief dread was that Raeburn would somehow detect her flight and swoop down for explanations.

Not that she did not have an adequate excuse. Anyone could see how ill Cecily was. But she feared that His Grace might have an uncanny knack of seeing other things as well, the desperation that surely must lurk in Audra's own eyes.

Bundling up in her own mantle, Audra hustled

Cecily toward the door. Just as she felt herself nigh safe, her worst fear was realized. Raeburn appeared on the landing above her, casting a long shadow down the curve of the stairs.

Audra didn't look back, didn't hesitate, but shoved her sister out into the night. Over Cecily's muffled protest, Audra fairly dragged the girl across the flagstone courtyard to where the coach awaited them.

"Audra," Cecily moaned, but Audra scarce heard her over the wild thudding of her own heart. She was moving so swiftly that she stumbled, painfully wrenching one slipper half off her feet.

Cursing, Audra had to pull up. Hopping on one foot, she reached down to right it, but at that moment she thought she heard Raeburn calling her name. Calling? Nay, bellowing.

Swearing, she yanked one slipper off, then the other one, hurling both the cursed things in the direction of the moat.

Able to move more quickly in her stockinged feet, she got Cecily to the coach door.

"But Audra," Cecily said. "I think the duke is—"

Audra gave her sister no chance to finish, part pushing part hurling the girl into the carriage. Shouting up to the coachman not to spare the horses, Miss Cecily was deathly ill, Audra vaulted into the carriage herself unassisted. As a footman slammed the door, she glimpsed Raeburn emerging into the circle of lantern light.

With an oath, the duke rushed forward, but his shouts were lost in the rattle of carriage wheels. Miss Masters's coachman whipped up his team, tearing out of the courtyard as if a thousand demons were in pursuit.

No, not a thousand, only one. Simon thought grimly as he pulled up short to catch his breath. He raked his hand back through his wind-tossed hair in frustration. Hands on hips, he watched the coach vanish into the night.

Now what the deuce had gotten into that woman? Bolting off without a word after having pledged to dine with him. Forever running away. If it had been any other female avoiding him, he would not have been surprised. But Miss Masters was not frightened of him. Far from it. Though not given to vanity, he had begun to flatter himself that she even liked him a little.

Well, the devil with her, he muttered, spinning on his heel. He could not stand out here all night staring after her like some lovelorn sot. There was a nip in the air, and some of his footmen were gaping at him as if he had run mad, which perhaps he had.

But it was harder than ever to steel himself to return to that ball. The evening that had begun to hold such promise seemed again unendurably flat. And all because she had gone. Raeburn was man enough to admit that. Miss Masters's company held great attraction for him, although at times he felt ready to throttle her. Yet they had been getting on rather well at the last. So why had she fled?

Perhaps it had something to do with that one moment when she had mentioned her former suitors. Her chin raised in defiance, Raeburn wondered if she had any idea how vulnerable she had looked when she declared. "I drove them all away."

Just like the princess hiding behind the wall of thorns. Raeburn had been teasing when he had said that to her, but now he realized that it was not that far off from the truth.

"Except, Miss Masters, I am no prince," Raeburn murmured frowning. "I am more of a dragon, and there is no blasted way you are going to keep me out." His jaw set with grim purpose, Simon was striding back to the castle when he was approached by a timid stable boy.

"Beg pardon, Yer Grace. But that last lady as what left here in such a hurry. Why, she forgot these."

The boy's eyes were round as saucers as he extended something toward Simon. When he saw what the objects were, Simon emitted a soft bark of laughter.

At that instant, Lady Augusta emerged from the house, slightly breathless. "Simon, I saw you go running down the stairs. Is something wrong?"

"No, nothing, Gus. Nothing at all." He astounded Augusta by planting a smacking buss on her cheek. With a puzzled frown, she watched as he strode past her whistling a tuneless song.

She was further confounded to note he had a pair of lady's dancing slippers tucked under his arm and he was smiling, smiling in a way that he had not for ages . . . not since Robert had died.

CHAPTER 7

The morning was well advanced, and Audra could not seem to rouse herself from the lassitude that had overtaken her. She had no inclination to venture down to the stables and go for a ride or even to walk into the village to see what might be newly arrived at the local lending library.

She might at least have delved into her book. The house was quiet enough with Cecily still abed. But *Ivanhoe* lay unopened upon the small parlor table, Audra not even possessing the energy to lift the cover.

Muffin had passed a bad night after leaving the ball, being sick several times, once in the coach going home and once in her room. Heavy-eyed herself from ministering to Cecily's needs, Audra had been left too exhausted to even think until now.

Slouched in the armchair before the parlor fire, she sat listlessly regarding what remained of the nosegay Uncle Matt had given her. The flowers were already wilting, a sad reminder of last evening's festivities. Audra had heard of some sentimental maidens pressing flowers into books to remind them of a particular night. But Audra thought she would as soon forget the event where she had made such a roaring fool of herself.

When some of the drooping petals came off in her hand, Audra chucked the whole bouquet into the fire, watching as it was consumed with a sharp crackle and an angry hiss. She supposed by this time the entire county would be clacking over her hasty departure from the duke's ball, wondering, speculating. Likely they would all conclude it was just another example of her odd behavior. What more could be expected of a woman who preferred books to men?

Far better that they think that than continue to link her name with Raeburn's. Hopefully, after a time, some fresh piece of gossip would divert their minds, and the mad spinster of Meadow's Lane would be entirely forgotten again.

And Raeburn? Would he forget? Likely he was quite vexed with her for running off with no explanation. At this thought, Audra nearly laughed aloud despite her melancholy humor. In view of Raeburn's temper, which rivaled her own, saying that the man would be vexed was rather like calling the conflagration that burned down the house a trifle warm.

But no matter how furious he was, he would get over it. No man could tolerate as many snubs as she had dealt him. He would curse her, but then he would direct his attention elsewhere, back to his task of finding a bride, filling the castle nursery with heirs.

As for herself, she needed only to put the events of last night from her mind. The infamous ball was finally over. She could go back to her own quiet existence.

But that was the very deuce of it. She was not sure that she could, whether she was destined to be haunted forever by the feeling she might have lost something infinitely precious.

Her one true friend.

Wondering why she should even be thinking such depressing thoughts, Audra leaned back her head, closing her eyes. She was weary enough that she might have dozed off for a few moments, but Mrs. McGuiness stepped into the parlor to announce she had a caller.

"Tell, whoever it is that I am not at home," Audra said.

"But 'tis your uncle, the Reverend Mr. Masters."

Audra's eyes flew open. What had brought him out to Meadow Lane so early in the day? She winced. Perhaps the old man had justifiably a few questions regarding what had happened at the ball last night. She had never thought the time would come when she would be so reluctant to see her favorite relative, but she wished Uncle Matthew would have given her a few days, nay perhaps weeks, to recuperate before facing him.

As it stood, she was not even given a few seconds, for he found his own way into the parlor. Somberly attired in black, somehow even his clerical collar failed to dispel his air of roguishness. The white waves of his hair were as ever neatly bound into a queue, the nip of autumn reddening his plump cheeks and nose. The familiar spring to his step caused Audra to eye him with some resentment.

No man of his years should be looking so bustling after having lingered into the wee hours at a ball. Especially not when she was feeling so dragged out herself. She roused herself enough to stand and greet him with a kiss.

"Good morrow, Uncle Matt."

"So the gel remembers who I am," the old man groaned. "I was beginning to wonder after being abandoned at the castle like a forgotten parasol or some other frippery to be fetched later."

"I am sorry, sir. Did not Jack Coachman explain how Cecily had been taken ill? I instructed him to do so."

"Humph!" He eyed Audra in a penetrating manner she found most uncomfortable.

"Truly, sir, she was. I have been up half the night with her. I don't know what could have come over her so suddenly. A touch of influenza perhaps."

"More like a touch too much of champagne," Uncle Matthew said as he made himself at home, settling into Audra's armchair.

"Champagne!" Audra exclaimed. "Muffin was drinking champagne? She has never taken anything stronger than lemonade."

"A girl must have her first sips sometime. Everyone must eventually learn to deal with the fruit of the vine." Uncle Matthew raised his eyes piously. "I, myself, have devoted half my life to the study of the brew."

But Audra only shook her head, this new information lashing her with remorse, adding to her burden of guilt. "I should have watched Cecily more closely last night. I should have taken better care of her."

"Nonsense. The girl had plenty of care. That Coleby woman was there, wasn't she? And Lady Augusta was most gracious and attentive to the child, introducing her to eligible partners."

"Did she do so? I-I fear I didn't notice." No, Audra scolded herself, because you were far too taken up with noticing the lady's brother.

"For my part," Uncle Matt said, pausing to help himself to a pinch of snuff, "I was glad to see you less absorbed in hovering over your sister and more bent on enjoying yourself. You did enjoy the ball, did you not?"

"It was . . . tolerable." She hated the shrewd look the rector gave her.

He heaved a deep sigh. "I wish I could say I thought that the duke found it so. But he looked quite glum, poor fellow. Especially at the supper hour."

"Oh, no! Did he?" Audra cried. Feeling a self-conscious blush about to steal into her cheeks, she turned abruptly to face the window. "I mean, I am sure that is a deal too bad."

"I never saw any man appear so pulled down," her uncle continued mournfully. "However his spirits seemed somewhat improved when he called upon me this morning."

"He what?"Audra whipped about, gaping at her great-uncle. Her uncle took an unmercifully long time about responding, being more absorbed in his snuff. Audra thought she would dump the entire contents of the box over his head if he didn't continue.

"The duke visited you?" she prompted. "Why?"

"Why not, my dear? Though the Raeburn family never attended my church, I've known His Grace since the days he was in short coats, although it has been many years since I had set eyes upon him." Uncle Matthew chuckled. "I believe he was agreeably surprised yestereve to discover me still alive."

"That does not explain what His Grace wanted of you this morning."

"Merely to talk."

Audra regarded her uncle as suspiciously as a general might one of his aides suspected of entertaining the enemy.

"Talk? Talk about what?"

"Many things. The scriptures, moral tracts. His Grace is a most learned man."

"And I don't doubt that he's every bit as pious as you are. Don't tease, Uncle. What did that man really want? Did it have anything to do with—"

She never had the opportunity to complete the question for at that moment the housekeeper bustled into the parlor, to announce that another carriage had arrived.

"Tell whoever it is that I am not at home," Audra said tersely.

"But this time, it is your aunt, miss."

Audra felt as though she were already up to her eyebrows with vexing relatives. "That's impossible," she snapped. "I haven't got an aunt within a hundred miles of here."

"Well, there's one whose maid is piling up bandboxes in the front hall this very moment, miss." Mrs. McGuiness said dourly. "Come all the way from London, so she says. But if you think the woman is an imposter—" The housekeeper shrugged, preparing to retreat.

"Wait!" Audra cried. "From London? N-not Aunt Saunders?"

"The very same, miss." Mrs. McGuiness smirked. Audra sometimes wondered if her housekeeper would announce even the beginning of Armageddon with such grim satisfaction.

Audra braced herself against Uncle Matt's chair for support. She could not have been more astounded and dismayed than if a bolt of lightning had rent her house asunder. Mrs. Prudence Saunders, here at Meadow Lane? Audra had little time to collect herself, only exchange a startled glance with Uncle Matthew before the lady was ushered into the room.

It had been many years since Audra's disastrous Season in London when she had parted from her aunt upon such bad terms. But her mother's elder sister still appeared as spare and austere as Audra remembered her, a veritable icicle of a woman, her fine-boned frame garbed in silvery gray.

Audra often thought nature had divided her gifts most unfairly between Lady Arabella and Mrs. Saunders. While Mama had got all the dimpled prettiness and too much of a zest for life, Aunt Prudence received more than her share of common sense and rigid propriety. So much so that it rendered the woman rather joyless.

Her eyes were so pale a blue as to be almost mild, insignificant. Aunt Saunders remedied this defect by frequent use of a lorgnette, which device she now trained upon Audra, subjecting her to a critical inspection.

It was absurd, but Audra suddenly felt all of nineteen again, gawky and hopelessly inadequate. She tugged nervously at her lace spinster's cap, smoothing back a stray curl.

"Well, miss," Mrs. Saunders rapped out. "I have had a long and disagreeable journey from London. Do you mean to stand there forever gaping at me?"

"N-no, Aunt I . . ." Audra managed to sink into an awkward curtsy. " 'Tis only what a shock . . . I mean, what a surprise to see you here."

Embracing Aunt Saunders was out of the question, but the woman did deign to offer Audra two fingers to clasp.

"Did you not send me a letter full of the most extraordinary supplication on your sister's behalf?" her aunt asked.

"Well, yes, I did." Audra refrained from saying that she had thought it likely her aunt had consigned her appeal to the fireplace grate. Certainly she had never expected Aunt Saunders to come swooping all the way down from London like one of the Furies of legend.

All the way from London? Of a sudden, the full import of her aunt's visit dawned upon Audra, what Mrs. Saunders's purpose must be. A wild hope stirred within her.

"Oh, aunt, then you *have* decided to bring Cecily out this Season. You have come to fetch her to London. I shall go tell my sister at once. She will be overjoyed."

"Not so fast, miss," Aunt Saunders said before Audra could dash from the room. "I have not entirely forgotten certain past disasters. Although I fully appreciate my duty toward my nieces, I am much more careful *these* days whom I take on as a protégé. I shall have to inspect the girl first."

Audra wanted to retort that Cecily was not a horse, but she managed to curb her tongue. She took a deep breath, reminding herself that Mrs. Saunders was Cecily's best, perhaps her only chance of a Season in London.

"Of course, Aunt," she agreed. "But I am sure you will find my sister quite charming. Not in the least like me."

"I hope so," Mrs. Saunders said frostily. She then leveled her lorgnette at the parlor, subjecting the comfortable room to her disapproving gaze. She drew up short, nearly dropping her glass when she came to the old gentleman ensconced by the hearth.

Audra had all but forgotten Uncle Matthew's presence herself. Usually so quick to greet any feminine company, sweeping his most courtly bow, the Reverend Mr. Masters had not stirred at the sight of Mrs. Saunders. Now he rose stiffly to his feet, made the barest nod instead of his usual magnificent leg.

"Aunt Saunders," Audra began. "This is my—"

"I know who it is." Mrs. Saunders gave a shudder of distaste. "We met before, at the time of your sister's christening."

"Indeed," Audra murmured nervously. She had heard some tale passed through the family of some unpleasantness between Mrs. Saunders and the Reverend Mr. Masters, but she had never credited it. Surely not even such an old rogue as her uncle would ever have been tempted to pinch Aunt Saunders.

"Madam," he said. "I would *like* to say I am pleased to make your acquaintance again."

But I am not. Her uncle might as well have added the words. His manner proclaimed it. After clasping Mrs. Saunders hand, he actually returned to the fire, holding out his fingers to the blaze as if he had been nipped by frostbite.

Aunt Saunders turned away from him with a scornful sniff. "And where is Cecily? I should like to see the child at once."

"Oh, no!" Audra protested, her mind filling with a vision of Cecily with her bloodshot eyes, above-stairs recovering from a bout of too much champagne. "That is, I fear my sister is still abed."

"At this hour! I hope she is not of a frail nature. I despise sickly people."

"No, truly, Cecily blooms with good health. She is . . . merely being fashionable. She has heard that in London all proper young ladies spend their morning abed, and . . . and Cecily always tries to be proper."

"That sounds promising. Very well. Then show me to your guest room so that I may rid myself of the dust of the road. I shall expect the child to put in her appearance by teatime.

"Certainly, Aunt."

Audra held open the door herself, eager to escape from the room especially as she could tell that Uncle Matthew was seething with indignation, ready to burst from the desire to vent his opinion of Mrs. Saunders's introduction into the household.

As soon as she saw her aunt settled into the cottage's one spare bedchamber, Audra instructed Mrs. McGuiness to fetch her uncle some port, hoping that it would put the old gentleman in a more mellow frame of mind so that he would do or say nothing to affront Mrs. Saunders.

Feeling rather harried, Audra rushed to Cecily's bedchamber. Flinging back her curtains to let in the light, Audra called out, "Hurry, Muffin, you must get up."

The only response was a moan. Cecily's muffled voice came from beneath the lacy white counterpane. "Please don't shout, Audra. I am dying."

Audra darted over to Cecily's wardrobe, rapidly inspecting her array of dresses. "Now what must you wear?" she muttered. "Something demure, but quite elegant, I think."

"All I need is a winding sheet," Cecily said. "You may have my best brooch, Audra. And give Uncle Matthew my miniature to remember me by."

Audra paused, long enough to give the mound upon the bed an impatient glance. "You must rouse yourself, Cecily. Aunt Saunders has arrived from London to see you."

"Upon my death bed?"

"No, you goose. To see if you are in fit state to be conveyed to London and gotten ready for your coming out."

"What!" Cecily emerged from beneath the bedclothes, sitting bolt upright.

"I suppose I must tell Aunt Saunders she has arrived too late, only in time to witness your demise—"

But Cecily scarce heeded her. With a tiny shriek, she bolted off the bed. "Oh, Audra, you must send Heloise to me at once with the curling iron. I've got to do something with my hair, and where are my sandals?"

As Cecily darted frantically about the room, Audra retreated with a wry smile. Never had a dying woman made so miraculous a recovery.

The wine Mrs. McGuiness served the Reverend Mr. Masters must have been soured, for the first thing the old man did when Audra returned to the drawing room was to demand when she intended to send "that woman" packing.

"Mrs. McGuiness?" Audra said lightly. "Well, I grant she is not always the most cheerful creature but—"

"You know who I mean, miss. That winged harpy from London. That Medusa who must have you already turned to stone. Meekly accepting all her insults, behaving like some milk and water miss!"

Audra stiffened defensively. "But you must see what an opportunity this is for Cecily, Uncle. You yourself said this reclusive life-style was bad for the child. If my aunt takes her to London, Cecily's future will be assured."

"And yours?" he thundered.

"Then I will not be obliged to attend balls anymore. I may actually find time to read again."

"That was not what I had in mind!" Fair quivering with indignation, her uncle strode to the bellpull and rang for the housekeeper to demand his hat and cloak.

"You won't be staying for tea, Uncle?" Audra asked, ashamed for feeling slightly relieved.

"In the company of that woman? No, thank you. I prefer my afternoon tea a little on the sweet side and not with curdled milk."

Barely pausing to shrug into his cloak, Uncle Matthew jammed his tricorne upon his head and exited from the lodge in a state of high dudgeon.

Audra sighed, regret at seeing her favorite uncle driven from her door mingling with a foreboding of the hours that stretched ahead of her.

But somehow she managed to scrape through the rest of the afternoon. Aunt Saunders, unaccustomed to country hours, was not pleased to hear how early they supped at Meadow Lane.

"And you employ a female to cook for you, Audra?" she complained. "I would have thought the time you spent with me in London would have given you some better notion of how to conduct a household. But there—" Aunt Saunders gave a shrug of resignation, that martyred expression Audra remembered too well.

Cecily had retired to change again for dinner. As Audra and her aunt waited for the girl in the parlor, watching the sun set over the garden, neither woman had much to say, which Audra feared was just as well.

She was relieved when Cecily finally did join them. The girl was looking particularly sweet with a ribbon catching back her blond curls, her dainty form garbed in tawny-pink taffeta. She had even tied an absurd little bow onto Frou-frou's collar.

The vision of such a perfect young lady should have pleased Aunt Saunders, but she merely pursed her lips, staring through her lorgnette.

"I have never approved of a dog being brought into the parlor, Cecily."

"It's not a dog, Aunt," Audra said, "It's a pug."

Although Cecily looked a little crestfallen at her aunt's disapproval, she hastened to say, "Frou-frou is very well behaved, Aunt Saunders, but I shall make sure you won't be bothered. I will make her stay over here in her basket quite out of the way."

Muffin was trying so hard to please. It would not have hurt that poker-faced old witch to offer her one encouraging smile.

It was worse somehow watching Cecily pinned beneath her aunt's critical eye than any agonies Audra had ever endured when herself a victim of that infernal lorgnette. But she struggled to curb her resentment.

Her aunt summoned Cecily to sit beside her on the settee. "So, child," Mrs. Saunders said. "You have grown a great deal since I last saw you, but happily not so tall as your sister. You have been living mostly with Audra then? A rather odd arrangement, I must say, but then I understand your late father was singularly without relatives and as for your mama . . . Well!" Aunt Saunders gave an expressive shrug. "So I suppose Audra has had a great deal of influence over your education?"

"Oh, yes, aunt," Cecily began, innocently unaware of the danger lurking beneath the question. "Audra always made sure that I could ride well and—"

"But for the last two years," Audra hastily interposed, "Cecily has been attending Miss Hudson's Academy."

"Indeed? I am relieved to hear it. And what accomplishments have you acquired, child?"

While poor Cecily stammered on through this inquisition, Audra found herself virtually ignored. She drifted toward the window to peer out at the garden. Not even the moon was out tonight, leaving the landscape beyond a black rustling void. It was the sort of chilly evening best spent alone, curled before the fire with a good book. Or if not alone, at least with someone more congenial than Aunt Saunders, someone less given to the fidgets than Muffin. A someone also disposed to read, or to talk about something besides ladies' hats, to jest a little or merely to sit and watch the fire crackle in companionable silence.

A someone Audra had never been able to imagine clearly until now. But the night itself seemed alive with raven-black hair and dark eyes, a heavy scowl that when it did lighten to a smile, was capable of warming nights far colder than this one.

Audra rubbed her eyes as if to dispel the image,

appalled by her own thoughts. The shock of Aunt Saunders's arrival must have unsettled her more than she knew. Or perhaps she had been reading too many romantic novels this past year. She should get back to the more acerbic wit of a Swift or Pope.

Trying to snap herself out of this peculiar dreamy mood, she was aided by her aunt's frigid tones. Mrs. Saunders said, "Audra!" What *is* that uproar coming from your front hall?"

"Uproar?" Audra straightened, listening, for the first time becoming aware of doors slamming, the tread of heavy footsteps.

"Surely, even in these barbaric regions you do not receive callers this close to the supper hour?" Mrs. Saunders asked.

"No, aunt," Audra said wearily. She did not even trouble turning around when she heard the parlor door swing open.

"Tell whoever it is that I am not at home, Mrs. McGuiness," she called out.

"Why don't you tell him yourself?" a familiar gruff voice replied.

Raeburn.

Audra's pulse gave a violent leap. She whipped about so suddenly she bumped up against a Greek statuette upon the parlor table and barely grabbed it before it crashed to the ground. Pressing her hands to still her thudding heart, she could only stare at the tall, dark man who seemed to fill her doorway. But she didn't know why she should be so surprised. His Grace seemed possessed of an evil genius for springing up when she least expected him. It was small comfort to know that she was not the only one so startled. Cecily gave a tiny shriek, and even Aunt Saunders dropped her lorgnette.

Swept in from the night, Raeburn presented a rather alarming picture, the black wind-tossed hair, the heavy drawn brows, the harsh complexion, the fierce, burning eyes. Despite the immaculate cut of his Garrick, he had more the look of a wandering brigand than a member of the peerage.

"Forgive me, ladies," he drawled. "I didn't mean to startle you. Your housekeeper seemed rather distracted by a mishap in the kitchens, some small excitement over a mouse caught nibbling at the Rhenish tarts, so I told her I could show myself in."

Aunt Saunders was the first to recover, seizing up her lorgnette, spluttering. "Upon my word, Audra. Is it your habit to have strange men running tame in your parlor?"

"Madam," Raeburn said. "I never run *tame* anywhere."

At this juncture, Audra managed to find her voice and rush forward to intervene before her aunt had a seizure. She stammered out introductions, but Mrs. Saunders appeared only partly mollified at the mention of Raeburn's name. In her rigid social code, not even dukes burst into ladies' parlors unannounced.

Lest her aunt believe this sort of thing occurred at Meadow Lane all the time, Audra added, "Of course, this is all such a surprise, His Grace never having honored us with a visit before."

She might well have saved her breath for at that moment, Cecily's treacherous pug leaped forward, panting, rolling her eyes with adoration, and scrabbling at Raeburn's boots as if he were a familiar and frequent visitor. When Aunt Saunders stared at Audra, she could only smile weakly, before turning her embarrassed anger upon Frou-frou.

141

"Get down! Down I say," she said, commands which, of course, the pug utterly ignored.

"Sit!" Raeburn thundered.

It was the outside of enough when that infernal dog obeyed him at once. Although Raeburn grimaced at the sight of the pug's bow, he bent down to scratch the dog behind its ear.

Cecily recovered enough from her terror to suggest, "She likes it better beneath the chin, Your Grace." She scooted closer to show Raeburn the exact spot.

"I doubt His Grace came here tonight to pet your dog, Cecily," Aunt Saunders said.

"No more, I did, madam." As Raeburn slowly straightened, Audra wished her aunt had left the man alone, to fuss over the dog all evening if he pleased. For now his attention focused on her.

Audra took a skittish step back, although all he did was look at her, one of his quick appraising stares. She had wondered if they ever met again if he would be angry or merely icily distant. But he looked so confounded . . . affable, except for that wicked glint in his eye. Raeburn was never so dangerous as when he behaved with an excess of civility, and Audra had a strong urge to place a chair in between them.

"In fact, Miss Masters, I felt obliged to call upon you, owing to your unseasonably quick departure last evening."

"I can explain that—" Audra began.

"No need for explanations, my dear Miss Masters. I only came to return something that I believe belongs to you."

Audra stared at him, but her incomprehension swift turned to horror when from beneath his Garrick, he produced her dancing slippers, a little the worse for having been tossed into the dirt last night. An outraged gasp escaped Aunt Saunders, as His Grace calmly set the shoes upon the parlor table.

A moment of the most awful silence ensued. Audra moistened her lips, a wild denial almost springing to her lips, a declaration that they weren't hers. They were far too small.

But Cecily was already piping up, "Why, Audra. Those are your dancing shoes."

The next time anyone came to call, Audra thought she would lock both Cecily and her dog in a closet. She felt a hot tide of color wash over her cheeks.

"Why, why, yes, so they are," Audra said, unable to meet her aunt's shocked and accusing stare. "You see I-I was obliged to take them off when I was at the Castle Raeburn last night. . . ."

That sounded perfectly dreadful. Audra swallowed and tried again, "I am sure His Grace could tell you, Aunt. It was he who first suggested I should be rid of the shoes. . . ."

No, that sounded infinitely worse. Audra cast an appealing glance at Raeburn, but the cursed man just stood there, his arms folded, a most interested look of inquiry upon his face.

"Cecily and I attended a ball at Castle Raeburn last night," Audra floundered.

"Alone?" her aunt asked icily.

"No, I was there, too," the irrepressible Raeburn put in.

Audra glowered at him. "My aunt doesn't mean that, you fool, er, ah, Your Grace. Sh-she . . . It was all perfectly proper, Aunt Saunders. We were escorted by my uncle, the Reverend Mr. Masters."

Her aunt shuddered at mere mention of the name, and Audra could see she was making bad worse. At that welcome moment, the parlor door opened. Never did Audra expect to be so thankful for one of Mrs. McGuiness's interruptions. The housekeeper came to inform her that the dinner was ready to be served.

"Is His Grace also expected to dine?" Mrs. McGuiness asked somewhat dubiously. "Shall I lay covers for four?"

"No," Audra choked out, at the same time Raeburn drawled, "How kind."

Audra's gaze locked with his for a moment. Twin demons seemed to dance into those tormenting dark eyes for all his expression of assumed meekness.

"Of course, I have lingered from home so long, I fear my own sister will have dined without me. But I have no wish to intrude. I am sure my chef can always send me up a bit of cold beef from the larder." Raeburn heaved a deep wistful sigh. "I shall bid you ladies good evening. Of course, there is no need to thank me, Miss Masters, for riding so far out of my way to return your property."

Thank him! In another second, Audra thought she was going to give him a mighty shove through the parlor doors, but with a soft cry, Cecily sprang to her feet.

"Oh, no, Your Grace. You would not be intruding at all. We should all be delighted to have you dine with us, wouldn't we, Audra? Aunt Saunders?"

Mrs. Saunders maintained a rigid silence. As for Audra, she muttered an oath under her breath.

"With so many charming entreaties, how could a man refuse?" Raeburn said, sweeping a mocking bow.

Audra half feared that her aunt might take umbrage, but years of proper breeding came to Mrs. Saunders's rescue. Although she clearly showed her disapproval of Raeburn in every rigid line of her frame, when the time came for him to lead her into supper, she permitted him to take her arm.

As the duke and her aunt disappeared through the parlor doors, Audra held Cecily back, hissing in her ear. "Muffin, whatever possessed you to invite that man to dine?"

"Why, Audra, he looked so very sad at the thought of having cold beef."

"The man is a duke, you little widgeon. His staff would serve him a seventeen-course meal at two in the morning if he desired it."

Cecily's rosebud lips set into a mulish line. "Well, I don't care, Audra. It was still the proper thing to do. Miss Hudson always said that a lady should behave graciously to all her guests, even the unexpected ones."

"Miss Hudson never had to deal with the Duke of Raeburn."

"He is terrifying, even when he is being polite. I suppose it is going to be rather uncomfortable sitting down to dine with both him and Aunt Saunders."

"Uncomfortable!" Audra snorted, for once forgetting her younger sister's delicate ears. "A banquet in hell would be as nothing to it."

But ignoring Cecily's shocked cry, she propelled her sister along, down to the dining chamber where her aunt and the devil were waiting.

CHAPTER 8

The tension in the dining room was by far thicker than the herring soup. Audra had never been troubled by indigestion before, but every bite she took seemed to settle into her stomach like a lump of cold lead. Perched on the edge of her chair, she kept stealing glances past the gleaming crockery and silverplate to where Raeburn sat at the head of the table. With each spoonful he took, she experienced a brief moment of relief. At least with his mouth full he couldn't talk, and she lived in dread of what he might say next.

To either side of her, Cecily and Mrs. Saunders sipped at their own soup in complete silence. Cecily's usual bright chatter had been stilled by nervousness. As for Aunt Saunders, she was too caught up in grimacing as she stirred her soup, inspecting it.

At last she pursed her lips, declaring, "This soup is too watery, Audra. If you persist in setting up your own household, an arrangement of which I have never approved, at least you could engage proper servants. You should dismiss your cook at once."

Audra didn't trouble to explain that usually she was so absorbed in her reading, she never noticed

146

what she ate. Her cook's shortcomings had never troubled her before, but she flinched when her aunt continued to criticize.

"This stuff is perfectly dreadful. Really, Audra, to be setting out such food for your guests! I cannot imagine what His Grace must be thinking, or what you should say to him."

Raeburn's lips twitched. "Knowing Miss Masters, she will tell me that since I invited myself to dine here, if I don't like the soup, I may go be hanged."

He read her thoughts so well, Audra nearly choked. But when Aunt Saunders stiffened with indignation, Audra hastened to disclaim. "Of course, I would not say anything so rude, Your Grace."

"Wouldn't you? Then you are obviously not yourself this evening, m'dear."

Audra's legs were long, but not long enough to afford her the pleasure of kicking Raeburn under the table. She had to content herself with looking daggers at him, an expression he serenely ignored.

Although he screwed up his face with every mouthful he took, he said, "For my part, I find the soup delicious. The best I ever ate."

"Do you think so?" Audra asked. "I shall be certain to have my cook send yours the recipe so Your Grace may have it every day."

"How considerate of you, Miss Masters. Just be sure the recipe is exact with nothing extra added. Like hemlock."

Audra bit back a retort. She could almost have enjoyed this exchange but for her aunt's outraged expression. Mrs. Saunders never made jests nor understood them. Although it took a great deal of effort, Audra fixed her attention upon her plate, pretending she had not heard Raeburn's last comment.

To her mortification, the rest of the meal was not much of an improvement upon the first course. Mrs. Saunders was quick to point this out, Raeburn just as swift to disagree with her. She found the mutton too tough. The duke said it melted in his mouth. Mrs. Saunders found Audra's choice of china a little garish. Raeburn declared the bright border so charming it even made the ragout of artichoke bottoms taste better. Her aunt insisted the roast of beef was overdone. Raeburn liked his meat a little burned.

By the dessert course, even her aunt had lost some of her rigid composure. Audra half feared to see Mrs. Saunders fling down her napkin at any moment and declare she was going to pack up her things. Audra scarce waited for the dishes to be cleared away before rising and suggesting that the ladies retire to the parlor.

She took great pains to assure Raeburn there was no need for him to rush on their account. "Enjoy your port, sir," she said through gritted teeth. "Take as long as you like."

" 'Til hell ices over, in fact," he murmured, quizzing her with those tormenting dark eyes.

Audra could have told him that it was in a fair way to being frozen already. One look at her aunt's pokerlike expression was enough to assure anyone of that. But she contented herself with a stiff curtsy, following the other two women out of the room.

No sooner had Audra entered the parlor, than Mrs. Saunders informed Cecily that the girl should retire.

"I am sure His Grace will excuse you, child. You need your rest, and I need a few moments *alone* with your sister."

Audra grimaced at the ominous sound of that, but she made no protest, for Cecily appeared quite glad to escape. After bidding a cheery good night, she forgot all of her ladylike graces and scampered out of the room, much after the fashion she had done as a little girl. Except that Muffin had never retired to bed before with such eagerness, Audra recalled with a rueful smile.

Watching the girl depart, Audra keenly envied her, being in no humor to listen to one of Mrs. Saunders's tirades. The door had scarce closed on Cecily, when her aunt commenced at once to tear the Duke of Raeburn's character to shreds.

"I declare that man must be quite mad. So disagreeable and such odd manners. He seems to possess no notion of his own consequence."

Audra thought that was one of Raeburn's greatest charms, but it would hardly serve to point that out to Mrs. Saunders. As vexed as she was herself with His Grace, Audra had to curb a sudden and fierce desire to defend him against this attack.

Her aunt continued to scold, "And your own manner toward him, Audra! Far too free and easy. Most unbecoming. Do not think me a fool. I quite see what you are about with him."

"You do?" Audra didn't think she was "about" anything with Raeburn, but astonishingly, she felt a hot blush creep up her cheeks.

"I don't entirely blame you."

"You don't?" Audra echoed, wishing she knew what the deuce they were talking about.

"The duke is, after all, possessed of an ancient

title, extensive estates, a handsome fortune. He must seem an ideal match for Cecily."

"For Muffin?" Audra nearly laughed in her aunt's face. "She is quite terrified of the man. Raeburn would make a meal of her. He needs the sort of wife who will box his ears occasionally."

"No lady ever strikes a gentleman. She finds some more genteel way of expressing her displeasure."

"I suppose a swift kick to the shins would also serve the purpose."

"You always did possess a most unseemly sense of humor, Audra," her aunt said severely. "However I am relieved to see that you at least realize the absurdity of your matchmaking efforts."

"But I wasn't . . . I haven't—"

"Besides being quite mad," Mrs. Saunders said, "I have never heard that His Grace has shown any inclination to be married."

"That is where you are quite out, Aunt," Audra said, smiling at the memory of poor Raeburn besieged at the ball by eager ladies. "He has been searching most strenuously for a bride."

"Has he?" Mrs. Saunders appeared skeptical, then thoughtful. "I suppose he is thinking of the succession. He is getting on in years."

"Oh, quite in his dotage."

Though her aunt froze her with a look, she ignored Audra's interruption. "That changes things entirely. If he is indeed marriage-minded, perhaps you did right to court his interest."

"I see. A half-mad duke dangling for a wife is more acceptable than an insane one who wishes to remain unwed."

"Don't be pert, miss. Small wonder that the duke

treats you with such shocking familiarity. Your own improper attitude has encouraged him. I am sure you don't want him thinking that you are like your mother."

No, Audra didn't want that. But why did it sting so to hear Aunt Saunders say it?

"At least one thing can be said for my mama," Audra snapped back, without thinking. "She never wanted for offers."

Audra immediately regretted the remark. She had long ago sensed that Aunt Saunders, for all her criticism of Lady Arabella with her multiplicity of husbands, had envied her sister as well. Her aunt, who longed to be elevated to the peerage, had to content herself with being plain Mrs. Saunders, the only proposal she had ever received.

As Audra saw a hint of red creep into her aunt's pale cheeks, her heart sank. Now she'd done it. Whistled Cecily's London Season down the wind.

The hand holding the lorgnette quivered, but her aunt replied in a controlled voice. "To be sure, Arabella did have many offers, but not all of them were respectable. I am sure we both want far different for Cecily."

"Yes, Aunt. I am sorry."

"Then we must strive to correct His Grace's impression that he may make so free in this house. You shall send Mrs. McGuiness to him, with our regrets. Inform him that we have all retired, but he may return tomorrow and call in more proper fashion. He will understand this subtle reproof that we found his conduct tonight unacceptable."

Audra rolled her eyes. "I fear Raeburn is not

given to accepting subtle reproofs, Aunt. If you have anything to say to him, you'd best do it more roundly."

"I trust I know better than you, Audra. See that my instructions are carried out. Being still wearied from my journey, I am going up to bed. You would not want me to feel obliged to return to London so soon."

Their eyes met, and Audra understood the implied threat. She must do as she was told or her aunt would depart at once. Audra didn't enjoy subtle reproofs any more than Raeburn would. But for Cecily's sake, she managed to swallow her pride and bid her aunt good night.

After Mrs. Saunders had gone, Audra had no other vent for her anger than thrusting the poker savagely at the logs on the fire. She raised a flurry of crackles and sparks that disturbed Frou-frou, still dozing nearby in her basket. The dog regarded Audra through one jaundiced eye, then went back to sleep.

"Lazy little bitch," Audra muttered. "If you had any spirit at all, you would have bitten that woman."

But then if Audra had had any, so would she, or at least she would have sent Mrs. Saunders back to London. Audra stared balefully at the peaceful-looking pug. That foolish dog was still wearing the ribbon Cecily had put there. Why did all her sister's girlish dreams seemed tied up in that silly little bow?

"Oh, the devil!" Audra said, feeling frustrated beyond endurance.

"Were you summoning me?" Raeburn's deep voice startled her. As before she had not realized that he had come into the parlor. Did that man never make a normal entrance into a room?

Audra straightened abruptly, the poker still in her hand. She might not be able to say all she wanted to Aunt Saunders, but that did not apply to Raeburn. Never mind her aunt's orders. She would send Raeburn away herself with a flea in his ear and take great satisfaction in doing so.

Mustering all her pent up wrath, she prepared to begin, but he wasn't even looking at her. He glanced around the empty parlor, saying, "What? I am to be deprived of becoming better acquainted with Aunt Saunders? And I was even prepared to fetch my cloak to ward off the chill."

His gaze came to rest upon Audra, the poker grasped in her fingers. "On the other hand, it promises to be a trifle warm in here."

Her temper sizzling as much as the flames, Audra slammed the poker back into its position on the grate. "Your Grace—" she began wrathfully.

"I know it is improper, but I would prefer it if you would call me Simon."

"There are many things I would like to call you at this moment, but that is not one of them."

When Raeburn laughed, she clenched her teeth and strove to begin again, but he interrupted once more, demanding, "What's that thing on your head?"

"Your Grace, I—" She broke off, raising one hand self-consciously to her temple. "What thing?"

"That lacy nonsense covering your hair."

"It's a cap."

"I hate it."

"Could we ever discuss something besides the way I arrange my hair—"

"Whatever you please," he said affably.

"Such as why you are behaving like such a confounded blackguard this evening."

"At least I, Miss Masters, am running true to my character. I wish I could say the same for you. If I had heard you mew "Yes, Aunt Saunders" one more time, I think I would have been ill from something besides that dinner you served up to me."

"I thought you said it was perfect." Audra gave an angry laugh. "Listening to you this evening, apparently everything I do is perfect."

"Alas, no. But I'll be hanged if I ever let anyone else say so, especially not that . . . that old, gray crow." He frowned. "What the deuce has gotten into you, Audra? I never expected to see you truckle to anyone."

Audra was not so angry that she failed to note his disconcerting but somehow delightful use of her name. "I wasn't truckling. Merely being respectful. Though it is none of your concern, I have need of my aunt's good opinion. She has a house in town, to say nothing of all manner of connections with the ton."

"What the devil does that matter?"

"It matters a great deal if one goes to London for the Season."

Though Raeburn's eyes were snapping with annoyance, his voice sounded more subdued as he asked, "You are going away? You plan to accompany that woman back to the city?"

"Not me. Cecily."

Was it her imagination or did Raeburn seem relieved?

"Poor child," he said.

"She desires it above all things," Audra said.

"And neither you nor anyone else is going to deprive her of this chance. So I am warning you—".

"Hold! Softly, my girl." Raeburn's tone was gently chiding. "I would never try to stop *Cecily* from going."

"You nearly did, the way you came waltzing in here, bringing back those dratted shoes. All your jests, the way you have been tormenting my aunt. You have given her the impression that I run an improper household. Th-that I must be a bad influence on my sister."

To Audra's horror, her voice broke. She was both appalled and astonished to discover herself near to tears. Raeburn muttered an oath, but she caught enough of it to realize he was damning himself, not her.

She scarce knew whether it was better or worse when he took her hand, roughly imprisoning it between his own massive ones. "I am sorry, Audra. I will admit I was annoyed at the way you left me in the lurch last night, and I resolved to have my revenge. I fear I carried my teasing too far."

"I suppose there was no real harm done." Audra tugged her hand free. She turned away to take a hasty swipe at her eyes. "Even without you, I would have run afoul of Aunt Saunders sooner or later. I always do. I never seem to do anything right, but for Cecily, I was trying so hard to impress her this time, to show her I had made quite a respectable home here at the lodge."

"And so you have. The place is charming. I have always been fond of it. It was once my older brother's retreat, you know." Having made this confession, Raeburn lapsed into silence.

When Audra dared look at him, she saw those

harsh features stilled into lines more vulnerable, and in his eyes, a look of rare sweet melancholy.

"Was that the same brother who . . . who died in the hunting accident?" Audra asked hesitantly.

Raeburn nodded. "Robert often used this lodge. Like me, he seemed to feel the need to escape from the burdens of being the duke for awhile. Of course, the place was more austere then. I can't even remember if Robert had draperies."

"You must not care for all the changes I have made."

"No, you gave it just the touches it needed. I was wrong to let it remain so neglected and gloomy after Robert's death." Raeburn gave her a half-sheepish look. "You will think me quite mad, but whenever I passed by on horseback, I always had the impression the cottage was frowning. You seem to have made it smile again. I thank you for that. I believe Robert would have liked very much to have you living here."

Fully aware of the enormity of this compliment, Audra was too overcome to speak.

Raeburn appeared to give himself a brisk shake. "But enough of these foolish reminiscences. I appear to have distracted you from what you meant to say to me."

"Which you know only too well how to do," Audra retorted with a tiny smile. "I am under strict orders from my aunt to send you on your way, not to let you return until you promise to behave better."

"I should not like to have to stay away, that *long*. It seems a pity I should have to leave so soon. The evening is quite young yet, with the others gone," Raeburn murmured, regarding her through half-lowered lids, "That leaves the two of us quite alone. I thought that we might . . ."

When he hesitated, Audra's pulse skipped a beat. Her hand fluttered nervously to her collar.

"Play a little chess. Your uncle says you are quite good at the game."

Audra did not know whether she felt more disappointed or relieved by this unexpected suggestion. But it reminded her of another grievance. "Yes, I gather you had quite a long talk with my uncle. I should think the pair of you might have better things to do than gossip about me."

"That was not my intent at all. I was merely, er, seeking spiritual advice." As he uttered this plumper, Raeburn concealed his face from her by bending over her chessboard. "Do you prefer the black or white pieces, m'dear?"

Although she was sorely tempted, Audra said firmly, "Neither. You know it is quite impossible for you to remain here when there is no one else present."

"Why? I promise I won't attempt to ravish you, not after seeing the way you can wield that poker."

"Of course I am not afraid that you would attempt anything so mutton-headed as that," Audra said scornfully. "But I have explained to you why I must behave with the strictest propriety."

"Your aunt must be sound asleep by now. How would she know? Your grim-faced housekeeper scarce seems the sort to indulge in a bit if backstairs gossip."

"No, she isn't. I don't think she likes Aunt Saunders above half." To her dismay, Audra watched Raeburn pull up a stool, settling behind the board. She made one last desperate effort to excuse herself. "I never play chess with any other gentlemen besides Uncle."

"Why is that?"

"Because most men sulk when they lose, and if I have to let you win, what's the point in playing?"

"Why, you arrogant little witch. Sit down at once," Raeburn barked.

Audra hesitated a moment more, but inclination won out. She drew up the opposite stool, saying, "Very well. But only one game, then you positively must go. Fortunately this shouldn't take that long."

But when Audra reached for a pawn to make her first move, his hand closed over hers, arresting the gesture.

"Wait a minute." His eyes were dark with suspicion. "After what you said, even if I win, how will I know that you did not throw the game on purpose?"

Audra smiled sweetly. "I fear you never will, sir."

"That won't do. There must be some wager, something that will make it so disagreeable for you to lose, I will be certain that you have to play your best."

"Name any amount you like, Your Grace, short of ten thousand pounds."

"I wasn't thinking of money." The gleam that came into his eyes made her wary. "If I win, you have to give me a kiss."

"What!" Audra drew back so sharply she nearly upset the whole chessboard. "H-how ridiculous. I won't agree to any such thing."

"Of course, if you lack that much confidence in your skill . . ."

He was goading her. Any prudent and proper young lady would have risen indignantly and pointed him toward the door. Finding herself sadly lacking in either of those virtues, Audra remained where she was.

Raising her chin in defiance, she demanded, "And just what do I get if . . . *when* I win?"

"Whatever you like."

Audra thought a minute, but it did not take her long to come up with an answer. "I want the freedom to pillage your library anytime I like."

Raeburn's lips twitched, but he extended his hand solemnly to her across the table.

"Done," he said.

He didn't even smile as they shook on it, but something lurked in his eyes that made Audra feel curiously like a lamb being led to the fleecing.

She settled back to make her first move. But her confidence felt restored as she observed Raeburn's manner of play. He took his turns quickly, shifting his pieces with appalling carelessness. Resolving not to be lulled into a feeling of false security, Audra played with more than her usual care.

While she debated at length between inching forward a knight or her bishop, Raeburn's voice broke in unexpectedly upon her thoughts.

"Do you mind if I ask you something?"

"Mmmm?" she replied.

"Why *did* you leave so suddenly last night?"

The question was asked in the softest of accents, but she was still considerably startled. Looking up, she stammered, "Didn't I ever explain? Cecily was taken ill."

"So ill that you couldn't even pause to say goodbye to me?"

"I-I am sorry. I know it was frightfully rude. You must have been quite angry."

"Not angry so much as disappointed. Supper, without you, proved a most tedious affair."

It pleased her, perhaps far too much, to hear him say so.

"My leaving was very likely all for the best," she said. She regretted she had not returned some more noncommittal answer, for Raeburn immediately took her up on it.

"Why would you say a thing like that?" he asked.

"People get the most absurd notions. Th-they . . ." No longer able to meet his gaze, Audra fiddled with the carved ivory knight, hoping he didn't notice the way her fingers trembled. "They might begin to think foolish things l-like that it was me you were fixing your interest upon. Utterly ridiculous, I know."

She waited for him to agree that indeed, it was absurd. She was further flustered when he didn't.

"I see," was all he said gravely. "And you would find such gossip disturbing?"

"No." She was too quick to disclaim. "Usually gossip doesn't bother me in the least. Unless . . . well, I don't like to be accused of flinging myself at men, being thought like my mother."

"My dear, foolish Audra. No one who knows you could ever think that."

His voice became suddenly so warm, it was like a caress, brushing along her skin.

"D-do you mind not talking anymore?" she faltered. "You are distracting me from the game."

He lapsed into an obliging silence, but that was somehow worse. His eyes never left her face. Dark, mesmerizing, they seemed to trace every curve, the line of her cheekbones, her jaw, coming to linger upon her lips. The parlor began to seem unaccountably warm. Audra could feel her brow go damp with perspiration, her heart thudding so hard she could scarce think.

She didn't realize how much her concentration had been broken, how much His Grace's own playing had improved until he said quietly, "Check."

Too late did Audra see the peril to her queen. Raeburn had maneuvered her into a position almost impossible to escape. If she could give herself time to clear her head, to think, she might yet find a way to win. But Audra no longer seemed capable of doing so. She could focus on nothing but how near Raeburn was, only the small table between them, the army of felled pawns and knights a most fragile line of defense.

On impulse, Audra reached out, making one last desperate move—the wrong one.

"Checkmate." In a flash, her queen was gone.

Her eyes flew up to meet his. The heat in the room became nigh unbearable. Audra pushed away from the table and stalked to the window, pressing her hands to her cheeks in an effort to cool them. Her heart pounded as she heard the scrape of another stool, Raeburn's footstep behind her. She sensed how close he stood, even without turning around.

"I don't like to dun a lady, Miss Masters," he said. "But there is the small matter of a wager to be settled."

"It . . . it doesn't count. It wasn't fair," she blurted out. "You did things."

"Are you accusing me of cheating?"

"You deliberately broke my concentration. You . . . you kept *looking* at me."

He placed his hands upon her shoulders and

brought her around to face him. "What a great deal of fuss you are making. I fear that is why I never play with ladies anymore. They take losing so hard." His teasing smile coaxed no response from her.

"It's not the losing," she said. "It's that ridiculous wager."

"Is one kiss such a high price then?" He lowered his hands, releasing her. "Very well, though I would have thought you to have more honor than to renege on a bet."

He started to turn away from her. Although Audra gave vent to an exasperated sigh, she caught him by the sleeve, stopping him.

"Blast you, I never said I was reneging. The whole thing is so extraordinarily foolish, but . . . but take your kiss if you want it. It's not going to be anything so wonderful. I haven't had much practice."

"Well, don't poker up that way. It's not going to hurt, I promise you."

Yet as he stepped closer, Audra could not seem to help tensing her hands into fists in front of her, holding her shoulders as stiff as the backboard of a wagon. Raeburn paused, frowning.

"Do you mind if I take off that lace thing? I can't bring myself to kiss a woman who is trying so hard to look like my maiden aunt."

Before she could even gasp out her protest, he tugged off the lace cap. Her curls at once tumbled free, despite her best effort to smooth them.

"There is a reason I wear that thing, you know," she said. "My hair is heavy, and the cap helps keep it pinned up."

"Yes, forever hidden away." Raeburn plucked

ruthlessly at the remaining hairpins until all the strands cascaded about her shoulders in wild disarray.

He brushed it back, his fingers snagging on the silken strands. "Did you know," he said, "That by candlelight, your hair shines with traces of a most remarkable burnished red?""

"You mean like dead leaves," she said hoarsely.

"No, I mean like flames," he murmured. Burrowing beneath her hair, his hand covered the nape of her neck. Gently, but inexorably, he pulled her forward.

As his face drew near, Audra closed her eyes, bracing herself. But his lips merely brushed across hers in a feather-light whisper. The contact was so light, so fleeting, it tantalized her somehow. Almost involuntarily, she uttered a soft protest when he drew back.

Her eyes fluttered open. That was a mistake for she found herself staring directly into his. She could almost feel herself slipping into the silence of his eyes. Her knees threatened to buckle, and it was a most fortunate thing that Raeburn was strong enough to hold her up.

For she became suddenly aware that he *was* holding her, his arms banding tight about her, crushing her close. His mouth descended upon hers again, this time hard enough to make her aware of his heat, ruthless enough to set the whole room to spinning. Long, lingering moments later, he pulled back. Neither of them scarce daring to draw breath, they stared at each other.

The sensations that coursed through her were wondrous enough, but seeing her own roiling emotions mirrored back in his eyes was like a miracle, almost more than she could bear. Still caught within the circle of his arms, she could not have moved if she had wanted to.

"Th-that felt more like two kisses," she whispered. "I only owed you one."

"Sorry," he said huskily. "I'll return one at once."

This time she didn't wait for him to bend to her, but raised slightly on her toes, her own mouth pliant, eager. She wound her arms about him, twining her fingers in the shagged lengths of his hair. Raeburn's lips moved over hers with such passion it was as if he meant to devour her. Far from being frightened, she embraced him in a manner equally as fierce.

Never had she kissed any man with such wild abandon. In fact, never had she kissed any. What was she doing? The thought, vague as it was, drove a sliver of sanity into her mind. And with the return of sanity came a kind of blind panic. She broke off the kiss, panting, mounting a desperate struggle to be free.

Although his face was flushed with desire, Raeburn permitted her to wrench away, his eyes hazy with confusion.

"Audra?" he said, reaching out to her. Even the way he said her name was enough to prove her undoing.

She backed away. "N-no. Please." Her cheeks burned with doubt and embarrassment. What the devil had gotten into her to be casting herself at Raeburn that way?

More important, what should she do now? She racked her brain for something in one of her books that might help her, some clue as to how she could beat a graceful retreat from this unnerving epi-

sode. But at the moment she could not even remember if she knew how to read.

Skittering away from Raeburn, bartering for a
little time to regain her composure, she began to
pick up the chessmen for want of anything better to
do. She almost cursed him when he came to help
her.

Although his hair straggled a bit over his brow,
he appeared more calm than she. "Did you want to
play again?"

Audra vigorously shook her head. "I never
dreamed chess could become such a dangerous pas-
time. Perhaps you had better go."

"Audra."

Her thudding heart seemed to go still as he
reached out as if to caress her cheek. It appeared to
cost him great effort, but he wrenched his hand
away, leaving her untouched.

"Perhaps you are right," he said. He gave her a
rueful smile. "I am sorry. It would appear I am not
to be trusted without a chaperon after all."

"Nor I," Audra said with chagrin. She could
scarce credit the mad way her blood had raced, how
she had pulsed with sudden desire in Raeburn's
arms, a desire she had never even realized she was
capable of. Perhaps she was more her mother's
daughter than she had ever been willing to admit.

It was a most dismaying thought and she felt
relieved when Raeburn moved toward the door. She
offered to have his horse brought round, but he
refused.

"I know where the stables are," he said. He
paused upon the threshold to glance back at her
with a thoughtful frown. "Audra, I hope that what
happened here tonight . . . well, it was only a few

kisses. Neither of us should react so strongly that we let it spoil our continued acquaintance."

"Oh, no, of course not," Audra said too brightly. She had no intention of overreacting. She was merely going to give up the lease on Meadow Lane and become a Catholic so she could retire to a nunnery and never have to face Raeburn again.

But apparently he read none of this in her face, for he gave a sigh of relief. "You and Miss Cecily should call at the castle tomorrow. My sister would be delighted to receive you. You can even bring your aunt. I promise not to toss her into the moat."

Audra nodded, only wanting him to be gone, to give her poor heart a chance to thud at a normal pace, her cheeks opportunity to assume some other hue besides fiery red.

"Good night, m'dear," he said. "Even if you didn't win the chess game, you are welcome to come pillage my castle anytime you like."

He upturned her palm, planting a brusque kiss there, then turned to stalk away before she had time to react. Still feeling his warmth upon her flesh, her heart a whirl of conflicting emotions, she closed the door. It was not until long moments later she was able to consider his parting invitation.

Come pillage my castle anytime you like. Recalling the intensity in his eyes when he had spoken, it suddenly occurred to her that he might mean far more than the library.

Dismayed she pressed her hands to her face. Never had she felt so exhilarated and terrified at the same time. Far from accepting his invitation, she intended to flee as far from the Castle Raeburn as a coach and four would take her.

CHAPTER 9

The Duke of Raeburn was considered to be un-approachable before he had had his morning ride. For that reason none of his household were eager to knock upon the library door to inform him of the latest disaster. The new laundry maid had man-aged somehow to dye nearly every last one of His Grace's crisp white linen shirts a rather dingy shade of brown.

Rundel, the butler, loftily declared the care of His Grace's wardrobe did not fall within his prov-ince. Bartleby, the duke's valet, suggested they all draw lots. In the end, Mrs. Bede, the housekeeper, was despatched to be the bearer of bad tidings. His Grace had never been known to hit a female.

When the trembling woman vanished into the library, Bartleby and Mr. Rundel were not above placing their ears to the door. The oak portal was thick, but His Grace's bellow had a habit of carry-ing, even through solid stone.

The two menservants were considerably be-mused when the housekeeper had been gone long minutes and no explosion of wrath followed. They stumbled back as the door opened much quicker than expected. Mrs. Bede emerged looking pale and a little dazed.

Bartleby, well-accustomed himself to the razor sharp edge of his master's tongue, inquired sympathetically. "Well, was it very bad, Mrs. Bede? What did His Grace say?"

For a moment, the poor woman seemed unable to find her voice. "H-he said it didn't matter, th-that no doubt there would be a fashion for brown this year and . . . and then . . ."

The butler and valet both leaned forward eagerly.

"And then His Grace *smiled* at me."

Bartleby and Rundel exchanged a startled glance.

"It's perfectly true," she cried. "And such a shock as you well may imagine. My poor nerves will never be the same."

Rundel shook his head solemnly. "When Betty carried in the breakfast dishes, she said His Grace was behaving queerly. The duke bid her good morning before he had even tasted one drop of his coffee. Of course, I didn't believe the girl."

"There is worse." Bartleby said. "I am never one to gossip about the master, but," he lowered his voice to a conspiratorial whisper. "This morning I fancied I heard His Grace *singing* in the bath."

The butler smothered an oath, and Mrs. Bede gave a soft moan. After which dreadful confidences, there seemed nothing more for the two men to do than lead the shaken housekeeper away to the kitchens to be fortified with a cup of tea.

Completely unaware of having raised any consternation among his staff, Simon had already dismissed Mrs. Bede's laundry report from his mind. Whistling a tuneless song, he returned to his task of rummaging his own library shelves.

Although fond of reading, he had never regarded

his collection with such eager interest as he did this morning. He pulled out volume after volume, giving each book due consideration, thrusting some back into place, setting others aside.

Richardson? Simon frowned. No, he'd wager his last groat Audra would not care for that author. Too mawkishly sentimental. Ah, but Fielding and Smollett. That was more likely. But no Goldsmith. Simon thrust *The Vicar of Wakefield* farther back on the shelf.

He paused in his perusal only long enough to feel slightly amused at himself. He should have been long gone on his ride by now, not spending his morning rearranging the library for Audra's benefit. It was rather a presumption on his part, this deciding what she would like and what she wouldn't. He had met with the woman fewer times than he could count upon his fingers. How could he claim to know her tastes?

And yet he felt he did, knew her well as if she had been spending every evening here, curled up in that armchair where he had found her the night of the ball, plundering his books, the firelight caught in her hair, the mists of imaginary worlds hazing her eyes.

It was a most agreeable image, and he had to bring himself up short. He was already behaving like something of an idiot. He had set aside enough volumes to keep Audra busy until her hair turned as snowy white as those idiotic caps she wore. And he wanted her to occasionally turn to some other occupation besides reading.

Like chess. He suppressed a grin. He should have been ashamed of himself for his behavior of last night. The wager had only started out as jest. But it seemed the jest was on him. Audra had kissed him back in a manner to steal his reason, and it didn't appear likely to ever be returned.

And yet he held no regrets, only a memory of how warm and sweet her lips had been. Audra consumed his thoughts, leaving him damn near useless for anything. He could not even seem to concentrate on the book sorting for any length of time, and he caught himself staring out the window instead.

If he lingered much longer, he would probably be riding in the rain. The heavens appeared so overcast, a downpour seemed imminent, but somehow even that didn't daunt him. He liked the pearl gray sky. It was the same misty shade as her eyes.

Staring, his thoughts miles away, he was scarce aware of the knock at the library door until his sister burst unceremoniously in upon him. He had breakfasted so early Gus had been still abed. Lady Augusta was already charmingly attired in a cherry-striped morning gown, her hair done up in a cluster of ringlets.

Before she could say anything, he strode forward and kissed her cheek. "Good morning, Augusta. You are looking fresh and pretty this morning with your hair all done up in those ... those bouncy things."

It was a handsome compliment to pay, especially to one's sister. She should have been pleased instead of staring at him open mouthed. "Simon, are you feeling all right?"

"Never better. Why?"

" 'Tis only that most mornings you scarce notice that I still have a head let alone how my hair is arranged. And what have you been doing to set the entire household by its ears already?"

He arched his brows in mild surprise. "Nothing. In fact, I flatter myself that I have been particularly amiable."

"That's precisely what I mean. Your staff is not accustomed to it this early in the day. Poor Betty's hands were trembling as she poured out my chocolate. And as for Mrs. Bede, I think she is lying down, with Bartleby burning feathers beneath her nose. You will be the death of these good people."

"I never realized being in a good mood was a hanging offense," Simon said. "If it will mend matters, I will contrive to glower at Farley when he brings my horse round."

Augusta earnestly suggested that he do so. "All this cheerfulness is beginning to even disconcert me. You have been behaving very oddly since the night of the ball. I don't think I'll ever help you plan another."

"I won't ever need another. I have already met the only—that is all the ladies that I care to become acquainted with."

She stared at him, her nose crinkling in a slight frown. "Oh? Have you given up seeking a wife, or is there something you are not telling me?"

"If there is, it is no fault of yours, m'dear. I always said the army should engage you to interrogate captured spies. You'd soon worm all their secrets out of them."

But she was not about to be put off by his teasing. When he moved back to the desk to rearrange a stack of books in danger of toppling over, she followed him. She studied him through narrowed eyes.

"You missed dinner last night, owing to some mysterious errand, and according to Betty, you took little for breakfast. If it were anyone else but you, Simon, I would hazard you had fallen in love. Can't eat, can't sleep . . ."

"It so happens I slept quite soundly," he said, trying not to look self-conscious. He had slept well, but only after thoroughly dousing himself with water to cool all heated thoughts of Audra.

"And you have not even gone yet for your morning ride," Augusta accused.

"You can see for yourself how threatening the sky is."

"Since when did that ever stop you? I've seen you ride in downpours that would set more prudent men to building an ark."

He didn't answer. He realized that he was behaving in a manner most unlike himself, but he didn't relish having it pointed out to him. Plunking into the armchair, he grabbed up the nearest book and affected to read. But Augusta leaned over his chair with the most annoying smile.

"If you are going to pretend to read, Simon, you had best select something else. You will never convince me you are interested in *Mrs. Pierson's Hints to a Lady on Household Management*."

Startled, Simon glanced at the title, then slammed the book closed in disgust.

"Your present state of distraction," his sister murmured. "It wouldn't have anything to do with Miss Masters, would it?"

"Miss Masters?" he repeated. "Why would you think that?"

"Oh, no particular reason. Only the way you

nearly flung yourself beneath her coach wheels to prevent her departure from the ball. And you kept her shoes for a token of remembrance."

"I did no such thing. I returned those blasted slippers when I went to see her last—" He broke off, but it was too late. Lady Augusta regarded him with a triumphant gleam.

He shot to his feet, pacing off a few agitated steps. "For heaven's sake, Gus. Don't start letting your imagination run wild. I've known Miss Masters less than a month. We quarrel every time we meet. I've only danced with her once, called upon her once, dined with her once and . . ." He expelled his breath in a sigh, heavy with resignation. "And I think I have damn well gone and fallen in love with her."

Augusta let out a trill of delighted laughter.

"Aye, go ahead and laugh," he said glumly. "I daresay Robert would have, too, seeing me so properly dished. Me, who always scoffed at fairy-tale romances, who could not stomach sitting through a performance of Romeo and Juliet. Now, here I am, behaving like such a veritable mooncalf, young Montague would seem like a pattern card of good sense by comparison."

"My poor Simon," Augusta mocked. But as she extended both hands to him, her eyes were brimming over with happiness.

He squeezed her fingers in a rough grasp, his mouth tipping in a rueful smile. "So, how big a fool does that make me, Gus? I think I must have loved that woman from the first moment I saw her chasing after that fool dog. Is such a thing possible?"

"Only your own heart can tell you that, but I should not be at all surprised. My dear brother, most things in your life you have done in a manner straightforward and direct. Why should falling in love be any different?"

She cast herself into his arms, giving him a fierce hug. "It was so horrid when I thought you meant to marry any female merely to have a duchess. But now, I am so thankful, so happy for you."

Moved and a little embarrassed by this display of sisterly affection, Simon patted her back. "Well, don't go wishing me joy yet, Gus. My lady is as likely to cuff my ears as to offer me a shy kiss when I propose to her."

Augusta drew back with a tiny frown. "Surely you don't think Miss Masters would refuse you?"

Simon was hard put to answer. Audra could be remarkably skittish at times, but she, too, was obviously given to approaching life in a direct manner. He was not a vain man, but as to her feelings for him, he had read much in those speaking gray eyes last night, to say nothing of the message she had conveyed to him with her kiss. Lost in his memories, Simon had no notion how much his expression gave him away until Augusta laughed and said, "Odious man. I can see you are not worried. You are wearing that obnoxiously smug smile gentlemen have when they are quite sure of themselves. So when will you bring your Miss Masters round to see me? I am dying to better make her acquaintance."

"I already invited her to call today, along with her aunt and sister."

"You what!" His sister fairly shrieked. "And here I am with my best afternoon frock wanting mending and scarce a scrap of decent pastry to be found in the kitchens. Men!" After which dark and incomprehensible utterance, Augusta bolted from the library, leaving Simon shaking his head.

He was at liberty then to gather up his crop and take his ride, but still he lingered, finding himself strangely without ambition. He returned to the window, the minutes slipping by as he watched the wind swirling leaves into the moat.

He possessed enough humor to laugh at himself, behaving like a starry-eyed fool, counting the seconds until Audra's carriage was likely to be seen approaching the drawbridge. At least he was not so far gone as to be seeing rainbows or hearing sky-rockets bursting.

He was finding love a far quieter emotion, like the warmth of a fire blazing upon the hearth on a chill winter's day or the sparkling glass of some fine, old wine. Although impatient for Audra's arrival, Simon's mellow humor continued far into the afternoon.

His household had even grown a little accustomed to this startling change in his demeanor. When Mr. Wylie, the estate agent, a thin nervous man, approached the duke, he tripped into the library with an air of rare confidence.

To be sure, His Grace did not look as if he heeded Mr. Wylie's report on the tenant farms with his usual strict attention. The duke sat behind his desk, fiddling with the feathered end of his quill pen, but he listened with the most remarkable patience and condescension. That is until Mr. Wylie reached the matter of Meadow Lane Lodge.

"And Miss Masters said she regrets giving such short notice, but she desires to give up the lease upon the lodge and intends to move out before the end of the month."

"She what?" His Grace thundered in much his old manner. His new-found confidence evaporated, Mr. Wylie fought an urge to dive beneath his chair.

"Well, I-I did not think Your Grace would mind. The lodge is so pleasant, it will not be difficult to find another tenant."

"The lodge be damned. If that woman is planning to go haring off again, I'll—" The grim threat left unfinished, the duke bolted to his feet. Wylie flattened himself against one of the bookcases as His Grace strode past.

His bellow ringing quite clearly through the stone walls, the duke could be heard demanding his horse be brought round at once. Trembling, Wylie cursing himself for ever believing Mrs. Bede's foolish story of the master's recent acquired affability. He hoped that Miss Masters was a young woman possessed of strong nerves. She was going to need them.

Audra's heart felt heavier than the parcel she carried as she wended her way back from the village. The lane seemed to stretch out ahead of her interminably, snaking past harvested fields and tall hedgerows. She had perhaps another two miles to cover before she reached the shelter of the lodge, and the sky above her waxed most threatening.

Yet she paid little heed to the gathering clouds, the relentless gray a perfect complement to her mood. Rather than quickening her stride, she trudged along, shifting the weight of the brown wrapped parcels to her other arm. She had had no real excuse for venturing into the village that morning. Cecily had no pressing need of more ells of lace and rosewater. Audra certainly had need of no more books. She hadn't even finished *Ivanhoe*.

What she had possessed was a need to escape from the lodge for a while, the clatter of her aunt's tongue, Cecily's innocent questions about the duke's departure, time to be alone to think. Uncle Matthew was certain to be cross with Audra when he heard she had come into town without even calling at the parsonage. But she couldn't have faced the old man's penetrating gaze, not after what had happened last night. . . .

Audra had slept badly, but she had hoped upon awakening to find that her sanity had been restored. It hadn't. From the first fluttering open of her eyes, images of Raeburn had danced before her, filling her with strange yearnings, quicksilver flashes of panic.

When she had chanced upon the duke's estate agent riding down High Street, Audra hadn't thought twice. She had impulsively informed Mr. Wylie of her decision to quit the lodge.

But now with the village left far behind her, balancing the unwieldy parcel of books, lace, and scent, Audra began to have doubts as to the wisdom of her action. Although she didn't quite regret it, she was more than a little ashamed. She knew she was running away. Absurd! Just because the Duke of Raeburn had kissed her. His Grace had no reputation for being a lecherous fiend. Despite his unconventional manner, his gruff ways, he was still a gentleman. She was not sure what his intentions were, only that they could not be dishonorable.

What truly alarmed her was that when she had been in his arms, she would not have cared if his thoughts had been a trifle wicked. She had only wanted his kiss to go on forever, and good sense, reputation, the world itself could all spin away and be damned.

She had sometimes wondered what it would be like to fancy oneself in love. It was every bit as giddy and feverish as she had imagined. She was behaving as badly as Lady Arabella ever had.

Audra winced at that reflection. She couldn't help remembering the time she had caught Mama planning to elope, run off from her fourth husband, poor dull Sir Claude Skeffington. Mama had been infatuated with an army captain, a dazzling individual with his bristling mustache and bright red regimentals. None of Audra's pleadings had been capable of bringing Lady Arabella to her senses.

Mama would have created the most dreadful scandal, but luckily, the captain had failed to keep the appointed rendezvous. Lady Arabella had been heartbroken until the end of the week when she had fallen violently in love with that poet she'd met at the Countess Lievens's drum.

The entire incident had been far more wearying to Audra than to her mama. It had taught her quite early on that sudden outbreaks of love were to be treated as highly suspect, given no more consideration than a severe case of the measles.

As for her own recent brush with what Mama had always called the "grande passion," Audra told herself she would recover. When she had left Meadow's Lane, she would forget this disconcerting interlude with the Duke of Raeburn. She would return to the peace and solitary existence she had always desired.

Yet far from offering her consolation, this reassurance only caused a cold lump to settle in the bottom of her heart. Never had peace and quiet seemed such a dismal and lonely prospect.

She attempted to shake off this lowering feeling and quicken her footsteps. It would be as well if she could make it back to the lodge before the rain commenced. She would have to endure another of her aunt's scoldings if she returned soaked. Mrs. Saunders was likely to be vexed enough when she discovered that Audra had gone into the village unaccompanied by her maid.

Bent upon hastening her steps, Audra scarce heeded what lay ahead of her as she rounded a curving in the lane. She was considerably startled when a blur of russet streaked across her path from the shelter of the nearby field.

Audra dropped her packages and emitted a gasp, more of surprise than alarm. The animal froze in its tracks. It was a small fox with a white chest, glossy red coat, and black-tipped brush. For a brief instant, Audra found herself staring into liquid gold eyes with a canny intelligence that was almost human.

"You little beauty," she murmured, catching her breath at the sight of the animal, but the cub was already scrambling beneath the hedges opposite. Before Audra had time to recover, she caught another sound above the rustle of leaves. From a great distance across the fields, she heard the "ta-tum" of a horn and the faint baying of hounds.

"Entwhistle," Audra muttered. She gazed anxiously in the direction the fox had disappeared, trying to gauge the animal's chances of escape. Beyond the hedgerow was naught but more open field. It was a long way to the distant outline of the woods. Unless the cub had a burrow nearby, it was likely to be overtaken. Of course on such a windy day, there was always a chance that Entwhistle's hounds would lose the scent.

But as Audra's gaze fell upon the parcels she had dropped, an idea came to her. She didn't intend to leave the matter to chance. Seizing the smallest package, she ripped it open, revealing the bottle of rosewater she had purchased for Cecily. Racing to the spot in the lane where the fox had first appeared, she uncorked the bottle and began spattering the contents.

The cry of the hounds was closer now. Audra could spot the outline of riders tearing across the field, hard. She had just enough time to grab up the remains of her packages and dart down the lane to find a hiding place behind the hedgerows.

Crouching low behind the thorny branches, she could soon hear in the road beyond a thunder of activity. Peering between the leaves, some fifty yards away, she could see Entwhistle's hounds, blundering along the lane, their din of baying petering out in confusion.

With breathless satisfaction, Audra watched the black-and-white dogs coming to a halt. Tails thrust in the air, noses bent to the ground, they snuffled the place where Cecily's rosewater had sunk into the dirt.

It was not long before the field of riders rushed up, Sir Ralph in the lead. His huntsman shouted out, "Hold hard." Audra winced at the way Entwhistle sawed back on his reins, pulling around his switch-tail bay.

While the whipper-in ran forward to take charge of the dogs, Sir Ralph was already cursing. "Damned curs! They've lost 'im." Not even giving the hounds time to cast, Entwhistle began to lay about with his whip.

When one of the dogs yelped, Audra bit down upon her lip, almost sorry for the trick she had served. Quivering with indignation, she started to rise from her hiding place, about to tell Sir Ralph she would take that whip to him in another moment.

But she was stopped by the sound of an excited bray. One of the dogs had sniffed its way past the rosewater and was setting up a terrific howl.

The huntsman seized Sir Ralph's arm, stopping him in midslash. "That's Flyaway, sir. He's recovered the scent."

"Then don't dawdle, you fool. Sound the horn."

To Audra's dismay, she saw the other hounds joining Flyaway and a mad scramble through the hedge commenced. As they erupted into the field, only a stone's throw from where she crouched, Audra tried to shrink down lower.

The huntsman was blowing out the notes of "gone away," while the whipper-in shouted encouragement. "Huic, huic, eu at him, my beauties. Foror-or-orrard."

"Oh, no," Audra moaned, already realizing what would follow. She shoved herself as far under the hedge as she could, the thorns tearing at her hands and bonnet. The ground beneath her seemed to tremble as the riders, hard after the dogs, began to jump the hedge. Flying hooves tossed up chunks of dirt coming dangerously near her. She covered her head with her arms, closing her eyes, holding her breath lest one of the horses fail to clear the hedge.

The thundering seemed to rage forever, but in what could have been no more than seconds, the fearful din began to recede. Much shaken, Audra opened her eyes to see the dogs and riders vanishing across the field without a backward glance.

Exhaling a tremulous breath, she struggled to a standing position and brushed herself off. Straightening her bonnet, she regarded the scratches stinging her hands. Well, that little episode had not turned out quite the way she had planned. But she had not been trampled, and perhaps she had bought the cub a little more time to make its escape.

Though still shaky, she fought her way back through the hedge to the lane, only to realize she had quit her hiding place too soon. Another rider, straggling behind the rest of the hunt, galloped toward her down the lane.

Audra thought of diving for cover but felt far too bruised to go through that again. It didn't matter in any case, for the approaching rider had already seen her and bellowed out her name.

Audra winced at the familiar voice. Raeburn. But she was more resigned than surprised. Of course it would be him. Was it not the man's mission in life to come upon her when she least desired or expected him?

As he reined in his powerful black gelding, Audra stared up into the duke's fierce dark eyes. Despite how dazed she felt from her own narrow escape, her heart did a foolish flutter. Raeburn made a much more impressive figure on horseback than Sir Ralph. So tall, the wind riffling the ends of his black hair, the storm clouds themselves seemed to cling to the broad outline of his shoulders.

"Audra!" he snapped. "Are you all right?"

She managed to nod as he slid from the back of his horse.

"Are you sure? You haven't broken anything?"

He ran his hands lightly over her arms. Even through the layer of her cloak and gown, she was too conscious of his touch. None of her bones had been broken, but they stood in danger of melting if he pulled her any closer.

Thrusting his hands away, she breathed. "I am fine, truly."

His concern dissolved into a furious glower. "You damned little fool. What have you been about now? I crested the rise of the hill a moment ago, and I saw some idiot female darting behind the hedges, right in the path of where the hunt would go through. I never imagined it would be you."

"I didn't think I could be seen. I am fortunate Sir Ralph didn't notice me."

"Fortunate! Was it your wish to be trampled by that buffoon and his infernal pack?"

"No, of course not." Although a flush of embarrassment stole over her cheeks, Audra felt obliged to explain what she had done with the rosewater, her futile attempt to divert the dogs.

Raeburn's scowl only deepened as he listened to her halting explanation. "You were following Sir Ralph about the countryside to sabotage his hunt?"

"No, it was merely an impulse." She stiffened defensively. "I know it sounds foolish, but I cannot bear to see any creature harmed, not even a fox. Just another of my eccentricities, I suppose. You wouldn't understand."

"I understand perfectly."

That was the devil of it. He did, perhaps more than any other person she had ever known. Those dark eyes of his glowed with such empathy, they seemed to reach out and embrace her, although he scolded, "I don't want to ever catch you taking such a risk again. If you did not already look so thoroughly shaken, I'd box your ears, my girl."

The possessiveness in those gruff tones should have offended her. Instead she felt her knees go weak. She backed away, stammering, "The danger is quite past now, so you need not concern yourself. I dropped my parcels behind the hedge. I'd best fetch them."

"Just one moment, Audra. I must speak with you." He caught hold of her arm and brought her around to face him. "There are some other things going on that I do not understand. What's this nonsense about your leaving Meadow Lane?"

She caught her lip between her teeth. "So Mr. Wylie has already been to see you. He didn't waste any time." There was no reason she should feel so guilty, but she couldn't bring herself to meet Raeburn's eyes. "I hope my decision to give up the lease doesn't inconvenience Your Grace."

"I find it damnably inconvenient. I suppose this latest ill-judged start has something to do with what happened last night—"

"I would as soon forget last night. That has nothing to do with my decision. It is only that once Cecily has gone to London, the lodge will seem so empty. Even Uncle Matthew has spoken of giving up his living, retiring to Bath."

"That rascal? Spending the rest of his days sipping medicinal waters with a parcel of elderly dowagers? You'd best come up with a better tale than that, m'dear."

"In any case, I see no reason for me to remain here."

"Don't you?" Raeburn's voice took on a danger-

184

ous note. A wave of panic washed over her, and she backed away from him.

"You'd best ride on, sir. It will rain soon. I must make haste myself, or my aunt and sister will wonder what has become of me."

Spinning on her heel, she set off down the road at a breathless pace. But it was utterly to no avail. She heard him coming after her. Short of running, there was no way she could outdistance his lengthy strides.

Leading his horse by the reins, he fell into step beside her. When she dared risk a glance at him, she noticed he was scowling, though more out of confusion than anger.

"Audra, what is troubling you?" he asked.

She wasn't prepared for him to speak to her that way, not in that quiet, almost tender tone of voice.

"N-nothing."

"Then why are you running away again?"

"I-I am not."

He gave a low mirthless laugh. "My dear girl, if I was prepared to let you, you would hike up your skirts and go bolting away from me faster than that poor fox fled Entwhistle's dogs."

She made no attempt to deny it, only hung her head, wishing she'd worn a bonnet with a larger poke to conceal more of her face.

"I realize my behavior last night was abominable," he said. "I am not very good at declaring myself. In fact, I suppose I haven't done so at all. But when I kissed you, you cannot be thinking that I meant anything dishonorable."

"Oh, n-no. I don't think you meant anything at all. It was merely a wager, a foolish jest. Pray, let us say no more about it."

"It was no jest then, and I am not jesting now. I want to marry you."

"Oh." Her hands flew to her face. Bonnet be damned. She needed a very large hat with a heavy veil. "That is very honorable of Your Grace, to be sure, but a little excessive. It was only one kiss. There is no need for you to feel obliged to offer me, as if you had compromised me."

"Compromised!" he roared, stopping dead in his tracks. "If you don't stop talking such fustian, I'll show you compromise. Damn it woman, I am in love with you."

His words sent a shaft of almost delirious joy through her, but she firmly quelled it. "That's not possible, Your Grace. You hardly know me. It's unlikely you could be in love upon such short acquaintance."

"It's unlikely to be struck by lightning, too, but we both know it happens. I am as fully aware as you how mad this all sounds, but I cannot help it. *I love you.*"

"Then I think you should go home and have a long lie down, Your Grace. Until you are more yourself again."

"Is this your way of refusing me?" He cupped her chin, forcing her to look up at him as he demanded, "Are you telling me you feel nothing for me?"

Audra thought it would have been much easier if she could tell him exactly that, but it was impossible, not when she was being held hostage by his eyes. "I admit I was also swept away last night, but no one knows better than I to mistrust such sudden emotions."

"Indeed? And exactly how many other times has such a thing happened to you?"

"None," she was forced to admit. She bristled defensively. "But I watched my mother fall in and out of love twice a week."

"You are not your mother, Audra."

"No? I'm beginning to have my doubts."

His sudden sharp intake of breath warned her that he had reached the end of his patience. But she did not have time to react before he seized her by both shoulders. As he hauled her roughly against him, her protest was muffled by his mouth coming down hard upon hers.

She struggled against his ruthless kiss, but it was to no avail. She was no match against his iron strength. And after a time, her struggles became so feeble as to be nonexistent. Even when his lips released hers, she could seem to do no more than murmur, "Please . . ."

"Now," he said hoarsely. "Now what of your doubts, Audra? I'm no rake, but I've kissed enough women to assure you this is no fleeting passion between us. I'm not asking you to marry me tomorrow or even next month. Just stay on at the lodge. Give us a chance to become better acquainted and then—"

"I c-can't," she cried. "I won't. I never wanted anything like this to happen to me. I have always been content as a spinster, to live quietly with my books, alone. Can you not understand?"

"No, I don't."

But this time when she struggled to be free, he released her. "I am not the sort to take a bride by force, but go ahead and run away if you feel you must. I can only tell you this from bitter experience. A book doesn't make a very warm companion on a cold winter's night, Miss Masters."

He turned upon his heel. Raeburn's gelding had used the interlude to wander away, cropping some grass. The duke covered the distance to his mount in long strides. Audra had a wild urge to call him back, but proudly, stubbornly, she pressed her lips together.

Seizing the reins, he swung into the saddle and brought the horse around to face her. "I suppose this is farewell, then? I could always tell Wylie to hold off seeking another tenant for the lodge . . . in case you should change your mind."

"I fear that I won't."

He stared down at her and slowly shook his head, but the gesture was more rife with disappointment than anger. "Strange, but I would have wagered most handsomely that you would never be afraid to throw your heart over. It appears that I did not know you as well as I thought."

With a final salute, he urged his horse into a gallop and was gone. Long after he had vanished, Audra stood in the middle of the lane, not knowing whether to cry or curse him. His parting words stung. He had practically called her a coward.

"It doesn't matter," she said fiercely. "It is as well I am blessed with good sense, Your Grace, since you have clearly taken leave of yours."

Her mind yet reeled with the shock of it. The Duke of Raeburn in love with her, asking her to marry him. It was mad, ridiculous, impossible.

"A proper duchess I would make." She sniffed scornfully. And if Raeburn were in his right mind, he would realize the absurdity of it. Someday when he recovered his wits, he would thank her for being so prudent as to remove herself from his proximity, before they were both tempted to embark upon some foolish course they would regret forever.

Buoyed up by these convictions, Audra returned to gather up the parcels she had left scattered behind the hedge. But as she recommenced her weary trudge homeward, such a mood of self-righteousness did not last for long.

This is farewell, then. . . . Simon's voice kept echoing through her mind until she almost wished she could weep as easily as Cecily did. It might have done her a great deal of good to be able to sob her heart out. But being herself, there was nothing she could do but keep walking. Numb at heart, she didn't even notice when it began to rain.

CHAPTER 10

The Duke of Raeburn was true to his word. He made no further effort to force his suit upon Audra. Nor did he attempt to see her again. By the end of the week, she was recovered enough not to start at the mention of his name or be tempted to fly to the window each time she heard the approach of hoofbeats in the lane.

As for the dull ache that seemed to have settled in her heart, she supposed that, too, would disappear given enough time and distance. At least her decision to leave Meadow Lane met with unqualified approval from one quarter.

Mrs. Saunders nearly smiled when Audra informed her that she had given up the lease. "At last, you are being sensible," her aunt said. "Now you may find some property more suitable than a hunting lodge; this time with a respectable widow to bear you company. Perhaps when Cecily finally weds, you could make your home with her. An elder unmarried sister can be most useful when one begins to have children."

Aunt Saunders proceeded to offer several other helpful suggestions regarding Audra's future, until Audra felt if she received much more of this bracing advice, she would have her first megrim. She was relieved when her aunt turned the conversation to Cecily's prospects instead, more relieved still to discover Mrs. Saunders had finally made up her mind. She would take Cecily to London with her.

Their imminent departure obliged Audra to set aside any plans for arranging her own removal from Meadow Lane. Wellington had managed to deploy his entire army with far less difficulty than seemed required to send one slip of a girl off to London for the Season.

Two days before Mrs. Saunders and Cecily were scheduled to leave, Audra entered her sister's bedchamber to find it a scene of complete confusion. Unpacked trunks stood open, while the bed was littered with hair ribbons, bonnets, gloves, muslin frocks fairly tumbling to the carpet. And neither Cecily nor her maid were anywhere to be found.

Sighing, Audra proceeded to fold some of the garments herself, laying them away in the bottom of one of the trunks. Although Cecily would be acquiring a new wardrobe in London, she insisted upon taking practically everything with her.

To Audra's astonishment, she discovered an old nightgown that Cecily surely must have outgrown. Setting it aside, her fingers snagged on the delicate lace trim, her heart snagging on a memory. Of a sudden, she could picture so clearly those times when Cecily used to bound into her chamber, a pale blond ghost in her white nightgown as she leaped upon Audra's bed to escape the terror of some nightmare or to demand to hear a story. Muffin's feet would be ice cold because the child never could remember to slip on her mules.

An unexpected wave of melancholy washed over

Audra at the recollection. She fought to dispel it, briskly folding up the nightgown, telling herself not to be a wet goose. She would miss Cecily, but it was not the first time she had parted with her sister.

And yet ... Audra could not delude herself. When Cecily had departed for boarding school, Audra had always known the girl was coming back. But this time was different. Aunt Saunders's remark had given Audra much pause for reflection.

When Cecily finally weds ... And, of course, Cecily would. It was the natural outcome of a Season in London for a girl like Cecily—pretty, of good family, possessed of a respectable dowry. Audra had no doubt Muffin would soon be betrothed, swept away by some dashing young man to a home of her own. Which was quite right, the way it *should* be.

Why, then, did it make the prospects for her own future seem so dreadfully bleak? Audra had always been so certain that she knew what she wanted. After all those years of chaos with Lady Arabella, Audra had desired nothing more than peace, the solitude in which to enjoy her books.

It had never occurred to her until recently that solitude might also mean loneliness. She had never given a thought to marriage until the Duke of Raeburn had stormed across her path. She began to wonder if she had been wrong to refuse him. If not his offer of marriage, at least his request that she remain at Meadow Lane. He had only asked that she give him a little more time, the leisure to court her, but the truth was she had been afraid to grant him even that. Unlike Mama, she had never been able to take risks in matters of the heart. Perhaps it was wrong of her, but she had always flattered herself in being so much more sensible than her parent. She was no longer so sure.

The packing forgotten, Audra sagged down on the edge of her sister's bed, propping her chin on her hand. She had never felt so confused in her entire life. Lady Arabella had been more like a flighty younger sister to her. Audra had always told herself that she was independent enough, she had never felt the lack of a mother . . . until now. But today, she thought she would have given much for the counsel of some older and wiser female.

Lost in these dismal reflections, she scarce noticed when the bedchamber door opened, until Cecily breezed in, slamming it behind her. Ashamed to be caught wool-gathering in this morose fashion, Audra bolted to her feet, briskly resuming the task of folding garments into the trunk.

"Oh! Audra, there you are," Cecily said. Her eyes and cheeks bright from some brisk outdoor exercise, she swept a fur-trimmed pelisse from her shoulders and added it to the pile on the bed. "Whatever are you doing packing my things? Heloise will take care of it."

"I don't mind," Audra said. "And as for your maid, her head is so far in the clouds these days, if the packing were left to her, you would arrive in London with nothing but a toothbrush."

"Indeed. Poor Heloise. Being but a country-bred girl, she is quite overwhelmed at the prospect of our journey."

"Unlike yourself. So sophisticated and entirely blasé about the whole thing."

Cecily pulled a face at Audra before turning away to her mirror. Her face flushed pink with excitement, she removed her bonnet and, humming, she snatched up a brush to smooth out her golden curls.

"I finished my last fitting at the dressmaker's," she said. "So I will at least have one decent traveling frock. Oh, and Audra, don't pack my lilac silk. I will be needing it when we go out to pay calls this afternoon."

"Not again," Audra muttered. It was but another of the disagreeable aspects of having Mrs. Saunders at Meadow Lane. Her aunt had wasted no time in receiving the ladies in the neighborhood whom she felt worthy of her notice and accepting invitations from them.

"I hope it is not the Colebys again," Audra said.

"N-no." Cecily paused in her brushing, long enough to steal an uneasy glance at Audra. "I-I fear Aunt means for us to take tea at Grayhawk Manor."

"Grayhawk Manor? That's where the Entwhistles live!"

"I know. I told Aunt you would not care for it, but Sir Ralph's sisters have been pressing us to call forever. Aunt Saunders feels that we should. Since Sir Ralph is a baronet and the local master of the hunt, that makes him rather an important personage. Pray, Audra, I-I hope you will not make too great a fuss about it."

Audra merely shrugged, saying she supposed she could endure it. Hopefully Sir Ralph would be out riding instead of there to sicken her with his hunt stories. It scarce mattered in any case. She seemed to lack the spirit of late to raise a great fuss about anything.

As she commenced the task of sorting through Cecily's fans, her sister cried out, "Oh, don't throw that one out, Audra. 'Tis my favorite." At which point Audra tartly suggested that Cecily might leave off fussing with her curls and do a little her-self toward preparing for the journey to London.

"I have!" Cecily said indignantly. "I have only just returned from taking Frou-frou for a walk, to accustom her to what it will be like in London, the streets so full of traffic."

"And what traffic did you possibly find in our quiet little lane?"

"A great deal. The farrier's cart passed us and Lady Coleby's carriage. Frou-frou did quite well until her barking frightened the Duke of Raeburn's horse."

Audra steeled herself not to start at the mention of the duke, but she could not control the quicken-ing of her heart.

"He has acquired a new mount," Cecily said. "Rather skittish."

Half a dozen foolish questions rose to Audra's mind. How had he looked? What had he said? But she gave voice to none of them, merely bending over the trunk, packing fans as though her life de-pended upon it.

But Cecily required no prodding to keep talking about the encounter. "I was afraid His Grace would be furious with Frou-frou. And you know how ter-rified I get when he scowls. But when he regained control of his horse, he spoke most kindly to me. He hoped I have a pleasant sojourn in London, and he even asked after you. I told him you had not been feeling quite the thing of late and were probably suffering from a touch of biliousness."

"You what!" Audra straightened so suddenly she banged her knee up against the corner of the trunk.

Biting off a curse, she rubbed the afflicted member. "Cecily! You know I am never ill. Whatever possessed you to tell His Grace such a thing?"

"Because it is quite true. You have been so pale and quiet of late. You never even bellowed at Froufrou the day she chewed up the binding of your Wivenhoe book."

"That's *Ivanhoe*, and it wasn't important. I daresay I would never have gotten around to finishing the book anyway."

"That is precisely what I mean. You have not been reading much, so you must be ill."

"But there is no need for you to go telling Raeburn all of that, Cecily. He might think that I—"

She broke off, flushing with discomfort, forcing herself to remember it didn't matter what Raeburn might think. She concluded lamely, "I am sure His Grace could not have been much interested in the state of my health."

"But indeed he was. He seemed dreadfully concerned. I think he would have called here this afternoon except that I was obliged to tell him we were going to Grayhawk Manor."

"Thank heaven for that," Audra muttered, never thinking that she would feel grateful for an engagement at the Entwhistles.

"I have been wondering, Audra," Cecily continued. "Do you know . . . I believe Aunt Saunders must have been wrong about the duke."

"Wrong? In what fashion?"

Cecily did not answer immediately, being more concerned with taming one wayward curl. Satisfied with her hair at last, she left off primping and came to curl up on the bed. She leaned forward in a confiding posture. "When Aunt first came here, do you remember that night His Grace dined with us?"

Audra grimaced and nodded. How could she ever forget it?

"Well, Aunt Saunders entertained some notion that the duke found me attractive, but I have been giving the matter a great deal of thought." Cecily wrinkled her small pert nose.

"Now, don't eat me, Audra," she said. "But I did just begin to wonder if maybe it was not you that the duke might be trying to fix his interest with."

"Me?" Audra croaked, fighting a telltale blush. "H-how absurd."

"I thought so, too, at first, but the more one considers it, it becomes plain that you and His Grace are monstrously well suited."

"We are?"

"Yes, you both make the same sort of odd little jests. He clearly detests large parties, and so do you. I daresay he would never object about your bringing a book to the table, nor mind your being so clever. In fact, I think he rather likes it, and you would never be daunted by his awful scowl or his surly tempers."

She concluded with a little sigh, "I think it would be just perfect if he were to make you his duchess and sweep you off to his castle to live happily ever after."

"What romantic nonsense, Cecily," Audra said. She forced a smile that was a little tremulous. "Happily ever afters are only for heroines in books."

"I might have known you would say something like that. Perhaps I have been foolish, weaving daydreams about you and the duke, but I do worry so about you."

"About me?" Audra echoed, considerably startled by this confession.

"Who will take care of you after I am gone? I mean make sure you are not forever straining your eyes, with your nose in one of those fusty books, reading so much you forget to eat your breakfast."

Audra was hard pressed not to laugh, but Cecily looked so serious, she felt deeply touched at the same time. "I shall contrive not to starve, Muffin," she assured her sister solemnly.

To her dismay, Cecily's eyes clouded with sudden tears. "I almost wish I was not going."

"Why, Cecily, you have talked about nothing but London for months. I thought you were so excited, so happy when Aunt Saunders finally made up her mind."

"I was. I still am, but I am frightened, too."

Audra wrapped her arm about Cecily's shoulders. "What is there for you to be frightened of, pet? You will have a wonderful time. If anyone was ever born to grace Almack's, it is you. I predict you will be the belle of the Season."

"I am not dreading any of that part of it. You know how much I love balls and waltzing and becoming acquainted with new people." Cecily fretted her lower lip. " 'Tis only that I have suddenly realized. I am quite grown up now, am I not? By this time next year, I could be betrothed, even married." She blushed deeply. "It is a wondrous prospect, but a little terrifying, too, to be trusting the care of one's heart, one's life into the keeping of one man. Do you not think so?"

"Well, I-I . . ." Audra stammered.

Although Cecily snuggled closer, she said, "Oh, I know what you must be thinking, and perhaps you are right. I am a goose. I did not expect you to understand, Audra. You have never been afraid of anything."

Audra found herself unable to reply or even meet her sister's eyes. She gave Cecily a rough squeeze and drew away. "Never mind, Muffin. You are but having a last minute attack of nerves. Your only fear just now should be that you will break poor Jack Coachman's back when he attempts to lift these trunks of yours."

This sally elicited a watery chuckle from Cecily. By dint of more teasing, Audra soon had her sister smiling and cheerful. By the time Audra left the chamber to attire herself for the ordeal of calling on the Entwhistles, Cecily was quite restored, waltzing about the room as she decided what bracelets to wear, all her doubts and fears banished.

Although Audra smiled, she closed the door behind her with a heavy sigh. If only she had managed to do as much for herself.

Audra expected to derive little pleasure from the afternoon ahead of her. By the time she crossed the threshold of Grayhawk Manor, she had begun to wish she had not been so lethargic, that she had taken the pains to manufacture some excuse to spare herself the ordeal of taking tea with Sir Ralph's sisters.

Her first glimpse of the towering main hall did little to rouse her enthusiasm. What once must have been a respectable Georgian manor had been turned into a veritable chamber of horrors, the walls crammed with hunting prints, deer antlers, and other mounted objects too dreadful to contemplate. Audra stole a closer glimpse at one such and was appalled to realize it must be a fox nose hammered in place with a brass nail. She averted her eyes, trying not to examine any other such trophies more closely.

Fortunately, the drawing room in which the Misses Entwhistle elected to receive their guests boasted a more innocuous decor—a few stiff family portraits and a collection of Wedgwood figurines on an étagère. At one end of the long room stood both a pianoforte and a harp.

Audra devoutedly hoped that neither of her hostesses would be tempted to favor them with a selection that afternoon. Both Sir Ralph's sisters had weak voices. Although they were not twins, they were both pale and colorless creatures, and Audra frequently had difficulty telling them apart.

When they came forward to make their curtsies, Audra was still not sure if she was addressing the elder Miss Entwhistle or Miss Georgianna. It scarce mattered for Audra was content to let her aunt and Cecily take over the conversation. Esconcing herself upon the settee with a cup of weak tea, Audra occupied herself with counting the minutes until this ordeal was likely to be over.

The visit was only enlivened when Sir Ralph popped his head in the door for a few moments. He had several of his unruly hunting dogs at his heels, but neither of his meek sisters seemed the least disconcerted at having these beasts running tame through the house, not even when the largest one gulped several biscuits off the tea tray.

After greeting Cecily and Mrs. Saunders, Sir Ralph wrung Audra's hand in hearty fashion, his bristling red hair standing on end like a wild red flame.

"B'gawd, Miss Masters, when my sisters told me you were coming, I could scarce believe it. Coaxed you away from your books at last, eh?" He gave one of his loud braying laughs. "You must have Georgy or Sophy show you over the house. One doesn't like to boast, but quite a place, Grayhawk Manor. Mentioned in all the guidebooks."

Audra managed to return some politely noncommittal answer. If the rest of the manor at all resembled the front hall, she felt she had seen quite enough of it.

But Mrs. Saunders professed herself deeply interested. She was quite fond of touring great houses, although Audra oft thought she only did so to catch the housekeepers out in acts of negligence, examining famous antiques merely to see if they were dusted properly.

The elder Miss Entwhistle kindly offered to escort Mrs. Saunders and Cecily over the manor's finest chambers. Sir Ralph held the door open for the three women, also excusing himself.

"I am expecting something to be delivered soon," he said, giving Audra a broad wink. "But I shan't tell even you what it is, Miss Masters. Quite a surprise. If it arrives soon, I may let you have a peek at it."

After this remark, which was clearly intended to tantalize her, Sir Ralph grinned and quit the room, his dogs galumphing after him.

Far from being intrigued, Audra supposed he must be talking about some new hunter or hound. In either case, she was not interested in viewing any animal that soon would suffer from Sir Ralph's careless handling.

As odious as she found Sir Ralph's presence, she

almost regretted his going. She was now left entirely alone with Miss Georgianna Entwhistle, a painfully shy young woman. Holding a conversation with her was next to impossible. Audra felt something akin to a toothdrawer, extracting sentences from the girl syllable by syllable.

She was glad of any interruption, even when it was only the Entwhistle butler come to announce the arrival of another caller. That was until the manservant made his stiff bow and said, "The Duke of Raeburn awaits in the hall, miss."

In the act of sipping her tea, Audra choked. Miss Georgianna's reaction was no less spectacular. Dropping her slice of bread buttered side down on her frock, she cried out, "The duke! Oh, dear, oh dear. What should I do, Miss Masters? If only Sophia was here. Should I receive His Grace myself?"

It was all Audra could do to refrain from shouting out a resounding, "No." It would have been to no avail in any case for the flustered Georgianna did not wait for her answer. She bade the butler to show His Grace in.

Wringing her hands, Miss Georgianna gave Audra a nervous smile. "S-such an unlooked-for honor. His Grace has never before . . . Well, he does have a way of appearing in the most unexpected fashion, does he not?"

"Like the very devil," Audra murmured. "In another day, he would have been burned at the stake for sorcery."

Georgianna looked considerably startled by this remark, but Audra was spared the trouble of trying to explain it by the arrival of Raeburn himself.

Of a sudden, he seemed to loom in the doorway, like the brooding dark wizard that he was. Audra stiffened. If there was anyplace in the shire she should have been safe from such a chance encounter, it was here at Grayhawk Manor, the home of a man Raeburn held in contempt.

But then, Audra could not help entertaining the suspicion it was none of the Entwhistles the duke had come to see. After all, Cecily had informed His Grace exactly where she would be that afternoon.

Audra's suspicion only deepened when Raeburn strode into the room. He bent over Miss Georgianna's hand, terrifying her with his gruff, "How do you do, madam." But it was at Audra he stared, one brow arched in inquiry, his eyes dark with challenge.

It was a challenge Audra felt unequal to meeting. Her heart thumping madly, she wished she had time to compose herself. How did a woman go about calmly greeting a rejected suitor? She was constantly finding herself pitchforked into these situations the deportment books never covered.

In an agony of embarrassment, she managed to get out little more than a curt, "Good afternoon, Your Grace."

When the other three women returned from touring the house, Audra took the first available opportunity to escape to the other end of the room, pretending to be deeply absorbed by the view out the window, although through the haze of her turbulent emotions, she saw nothing.

Neither the misses Entwhistle nor Cecily were forceful enough to keep Raeburn engaged in conversation, but Audra assumed that her aunt would be. She was wrong. On the pretext of bringing her another cup of tea, Raeburn joined her at the window.

"Attempting to cut my acquaintance, Miss Masters?" he drawled softly.

"N-no," she stammered. "I was merely admiring the view. There is the most charming . . ." She paused, squinting past the curtains. Exactly what was out there?

"Stables, Miss Masters. They are called stables. It is where the horses are kept." With a wry half smile, he offered her the cup and saucer, but she shook her head. Her hands were trembling so badly, she did not dare accept it.

He set the china down while she played nervously with the lace at the throat of her gown. She could not bring herself to look at him, but she was all too aware of his presence, how close he stood. It was an idiotic thing to be realizing at this particular moment, but how much she had missed the wretched man these past days, the gruff sound of his voice.

"How astonishing to see *you* here this afternoon," she said to cover her own confusion. "I know Sir Ralph is not exactly a favorite of yours."

"Nor yours either," he reminded her. "Myself, I felt the need of a little company. It is rather dull at the castle. My sister returned to Hampstead yesterday, you know."

"No, I had not heard."

"I fear Gus left rather disheartened. All that effort she put into hostessing that ball to see me legshackled to some proper young lady, and now, not a prospective duchess to show for it."

"Lady Augusta can scarce blame you for that. I am sure you did your best to . . . to find a bride."

"Did I? I am beginning to think I might have

given up far too easily. You look very pale, Audra. Your sister tells me you have been ill."

"Cecily is a goose!" she said with a fierce blush, then admitted reluctantly, "Perhaps I have been feeling a little strange of late. But 'tis nothing fatal, I assure you. I will recover."

"Likely you will, m'dear. But why do you want to?"

Glancing up, her eyes locked with his, and for a moment, Audra could not recollect the reason herself. The conversation seemed to have slipped into very dangerous channels. Wrenching her gaze away, she took a step back murmuring, "Perhaps we should both return to our seats, Your Grace. I fear my aunt is staring at us."

This was perfectly true. Mrs. Saunders had trained her lorgnette upon their tête-à-tête with a disapproving frown. Skirting past Raeburn, Audra resumed her place among the other ladies.

Simon made no immediate effort to follow suit. Silently cursing himself for a fool, he thought that he should never have come to Grayhawk Manor. He had only decided to do so earlier that day after he had spoken with Cecily in the lane. The girl's innocent prattle had let slip the interesting fact that Audra had been behaving in ways most unlike herself of late.

Indeed she must be to ever consider crossing Sir Ralph's threshold, a man she quite detested. Since Audra's rejection of his suit, stubborn pride had kept Simon from pursuing her any further. But Cecily's report of her sister's listless manner had intrigued him, given him cause for hope. Enough so that he felt he must see Audra again.

One look into her eyes had told him she'd been as miserable as he these past days. But at his gentle probing, he had watched the familiar alarm chase across her features, making her once more ready to bolt.

Perhaps he had turned out to be a very poor dragon after all, so easily turned aside by her wall of thorns. But he knew he could be as fierce and demanding as he pleased, but to no avail. There were some fears the lady could only conquer herself.

He had accomplished nothing by coming here except perhaps to stir the embers of his own frustration and disappointment. Consequently he prepared to take his leave when the parlor door opened to admit Sir Ralph.

The baronet's portly features were flushed red with excitement. "B'gawd, it has arrived. You must all come out at once."

Simon did not have the damnedest notion what *it* was, nor much interest in finding out. But Sir Ralph clearly meant to give none of them any peace until they had all trooped outside to view his latest acquisition.

While the ladies gathered up their shawls, Simon retrieved his own Garrick and high-crowned hat from the butler. Sir Ralph led them out to the front of the house. Simon perceived nothing remarkable, only a horse and cart pulled to on the gravel drive. Sir Ralph's huntsman was unloading what appeared to be a small cage from the back of the cart.

Upon closer inspection, Simon realized that cowering behind the wire mesh was a small silver-gray fox, the cub's large liquid eyes wide with terror.

"Oh, how sweet," cooed Cecily.

"Vermin!" Mrs. Saunders shuddered.

"No, a *vixen*," Sir Ralph said. "Confiscated it from one of my tenants. The demned fool had found an entire litter of foxes abandoned and never told me. This is the only one survived and he was letting his daughter keep it as a pet. Of all the nonsense."

The baronet chuckled, giving Simon a nudge. "After this beauty's raised to be a mite bigger, the little vixen should provide my hounds with some good sport, eh, Your Grace?"

Raeburn vouchsafed no answer, merely glowering in disgust at Entwhistle's notion of sport. But disgust was too mild a word to apply to Audra's reaction. She turned quite pale, the stricken look in her eyes not much different from the vixen trapped within the cage.

Shivering in the chill November air, the other ladies soon lost interest and returned to the drawing room. Sir Ralph had stepped round to the front of the cart to deliver some instructions regarding the disposition of the fox to his huntsman.

But Audra bit down upon her lip, seeming unable to tear herself away. As her head came slowly up, never had she appeared so vulnerable, her gaze meeting Simon's in mute appeal.

He swore under his breath, knowing he was about to make a great cake of himself. He would be lucky if that fool Entwhistle did not have a fit of apoplexy, but he hunkered down anyway and began to undo the latch of the cage.

The fox crouched away from him in fear. Simon proceeded with caution. Even if the vixen had been raised as a pet, it was still a thing of the wilds.

"Oh, be careful. She might bite you," Audra said,

bending down beside him. "Here, take my shawl."

Whipping it from her shoulders, she handed him the soft length of wool. Simon managed to catch the vixen up in the bright folds. Although the animal trembled and shivered, it offered no resistance.

As he placed the bundled cub into Audra's eager outstretched hands, Simon had his reward. For the first time since she had rejected his proposal, she smiled at him.

Raeburn was not given long to bask in the moment for Sir Ralph had become aware that some mischief was afoot.

"What the deuce!" he shouted, coming round the side of the cart. Simon prepared to head him off, but he saw Audra straighten, the spark of fire coming into her eyes and knew that Entwhistle was about to receive the trimming of his life.

"What the blazes are you planning to do with my fox, Miss Masters?" Sir Ralph demanded with a scowl.

"Run," she gasped out.

This strange answer was not the furious response that Raeburn had expected, any more than the look of panic that overtook her. But he fast saw the reason for this sudden change in expression. It was not inspired by fear of Entwhistle but of three large hounds that came loping up from the stableyard.

On such a cold, cloudy day, the scent of fox carried quite clearly. The dogs would have no difficulty locating their prey, even if the terrified vixen had not been peeking out from the folds of the shawl.

With a loud baying, the hounds charged in Audra's direction. She turned to flee, attempting to hold the cub high out of reach. Raeburn managed to collar one of the dogs, but Sir Ralph's cursing and kicking out with his thick boots only made the situation worse.

Audra feared the wisest course might have been to return the fox to the safety of its cage, but it was too late for that now. One of the dogs was already leaping at her skirts. Her only escape seemed to lie in the direction of the house.

Stumbling up the steps, beneath the portico of the gray stone Georgian manor, she heard Raeburn's shouts behind her above the din of the dogs and Sir Ralph's bellows. But the undisciplined hounds heeded neither of the two men.

With a mighty jump, the largest dog caught the end of the shawl in its powerful jaws. Audra shoved frantically at the manor's heavy oak door, stumbling inside. As she sought to bar the dogs entry, the terrified vixen sank its teeth into Audra's hand.

She cried out at the sharp pain, dropping both shawl and fox, letting the door swing wide. The animal streaked across the hall in a blur of gray, the dogs hard after it. It was unfortunate that Mrs. Saunders chose that particular moment to fling open the drawing room door, demanding, "What is this unseemly—"

Her sentence trailed off in a gasp as the fox shot past her skirts. She had no time to recover before the two dogs rushed forward, knocking her over in their frantic haste.

The pandemonium that followed would remain forever a merciful blur in Audra's mind. She would recollect nothing but a scene of confusion, shrieking women, shattering china, barking dogs.

How long the chaos might have continued she did not know, except that Raeburn had the presence of mind to fling open a window, offering the fox an avenue of escape. With the aid of Sir Ralph's huntsman, he got the dogs under control and removed from the parlor.

Only then did Audra fully realize what a fright she had had. She sank down into an armchair, trembling, clutching her injured hand. Grimacing, she surveyed the disaster that was the drawing room. Bits of broken saucers were strewn everywhere, tables overturned, tea soaking a stain into the carpet. The elder Miss Entwhistle lay moaning upon the settee while Cecily and Georgianna strove to revive her with smelling salts. Aunt Saunders pursed her lips, staring at the muddied paw prints on her gown.

The only one who appeared calm was Raeburn. He produced his handkerchief and stanched the trickle of blood escaping from Audra's wound.

"Fetch me some brandy, Entwhistle," he snapped.

But Sir Ralph was too preoccupied lamenting the loss of his fox. "B'gawd, sir," he bawled. "You've cost me one of the likeliest little vixens I ever saw. I should call you out for this. So I should."

But one black look from Raeburn put a stop to the baronet's bluster. Unfortunately Mrs. Saunders was not so easily silenced. As soon as she had recovered from her shock, she rounded upon Audra in an icy fury.

"You! You are to blame for this vulgar incident."

"The fault lies more with me, madam," Raeburn began, but Mrs. Saunders took no heed of him, continuing to lash out at Audra.

"This was all a malicious jest, another example of your coarse sense of humor. You set those dogs in here on purpose."

"Of course, I did not, Aunt," Audra said wearily.

"I thought you had finally changed, abandoned your odd ways, acquired some notion of proper conduct. But you still have no more notion how to be a lady than the veriest trollop. Any more so than your mama ever had. I completely wash my hands of you this time. I never intend to set foot beneath any roof that harbors you again."

Audra heard Raeburn draw in an angry breath, but before he could say anything, she placed her hand firmly on his, giving a warning squeeze.

"I quite understand, Aunt Saunders," she faltered. "But you will not hold this against Cecily? You will still take her to London?"

"Of course. If for no other reason than to remove the child from your deplorable sphere of influence."

"Well, I won't go!" Cecily's sudden passionate declaration startled them all, rendering even Mrs. Saunders momentarily speechless. The girl straightened from bending over Miss Entwhistle. Cecily's delicate features were flushed.

"Muffin . . ." Audra tried to caution her, but she had never seen her younger sister tremble with such indignation.

Tears stinging her blue eyes, Cecily stomped her small foot. "You have done nothing but insult my sister ever since you came to Meadow Lane, Aunt Saunders, and I am wearied of it. If you are going to be this mean to Audra, I wish that you had never come to visit us, never invited me to your house."

Mrs. Saunders's lips thinned, her eyes turning to slivers of ice. "Your wish is easily granted, child."

In a state of high dudgeon, she stalked from the room. Raeburn whistled softly under his breath, eying Cecily with admiration. Audra had to swallow past a lump in her throat. Although she was deeply moved by her sister's unexpected championship, she could not help exclaiming, "Oh, Muffin! What *have* you done?"

Cecily gave a shrug that was a shade too careless. " 'Tis of no consequence, Audra. Who wanted to go to dull old London anyway?"

After which heroic declaration, she burst into tears and sank down, burying her face in Audra's lap.

CHAPTER 11

Upon her return to Meadow Lane Lodge, Mrs. Saunders wasted no time in gathering up her maid and her belongings. She would not spend so much as another night in the company of such ungrateful hoydens as both her nieces had shown themselves to be. Drained herself by the day's events, Audra made no effort to dissuade her.

She was far too preoccupied with soothing Cecily. Suffering from a state of overexcitement and keen disappointment, the girl had wept herself into a megrim. After administering some hartshorn to her sister, Audra felt relieved when Cecily drifted off to sleep.

She was not on hand to witness Mrs. Saunders's departure. The sky had just darkened to a shade of deep purple when that outraged lady flounced out to her carriage. Audra very civilly accompanied her, waiting until she saw her aunt safely bestowed inside the coach, although Mrs. Saunders refused to even bid her farewell.

Audra stepped back as the coachman whipped up the team. The carriage had not even reached the bend in the lane when the Duke of Raeburn's mount galloped into sight. Raeburn cheerfully tipped his hat to the passing coach, a gesture that,

Audra was certain, went quite unacknowledged.

She lingered on her doorstep, watching the duke's approach, for once not surprised to see him. Somehow she had known he would come to her this evening.

He drew rein in front of the cottage, the wind whipping at the ends of his riding cape. As he stared down at her, his half smile glinted in the gathering dusk.

"I take it you are at home this time, Miss Masters?"

"I believe so, Your Grace," she said demurely.

Dismounting, he consigned his horse to the care of one of her grooms, then followed Audra inside. Mrs. McGuiness sniffed with disapproval to discover that Audra had usurped her prerogative of admitting visitors, but she bustled away to fetch refreshments to the parlor.

Still chilled from being out of doors without her shawl, Audra stepped near the fire, holding out her hands to the blaze to warm them. Although very conscious of Raeburn's nearness, she felt strangely calm.

"I saw your aunt leaving posthaste," the duke remarked. "Such dire consequences of our little adventure this afternoon. Do you know that Sir Ralph has vowed never to invite either of us to tea again?"

A wry smile escaped Audra. "I think we shall manage to survive."

"How is your hand?" he asked, stepping closer. "You must take care not to let it become infected. Does it still hurt?"

Audra shook her head. Her calm threatened to desert her at the prospect of his touch. But she made no movement to pull away when he took her hand, examining the bandagings wrapped about her wrist.

Raeburn swore softly. "I am sorry, Audra. The entire disaster was all my doing. If I had not removed that blasted fox from its cage—"

"You only did so to please me. I doubt one man in a hundred would understand my foolish tender-heartedness toward animals. And you are the only one I know who would have acted upon it."

"I suppose that makes us both quite mad."

"Perhaps we are. Cecily says—" She broke off, blushing a little.

"Yes?" he prompted.

"She says that we are well matched."

"What a wise child."

"A most unhappy one. That is my one regret about what happened today. I don't care a fig for the Entwhistles or my aunt's goodwill. But I do feel so wretched about being the cause of Cecily's losing her London Season."

"There is a solution to the problem."

"Don't suggest that I write to my mother. You must know as well as I how futile—"

"I was thinking more about my sister."

"Lady Augusta?"

"You have no notion how fond Gus is of playing matchmaker. It would give her the greatest delight to sponsor your sister. Such a treat might even make up to her for all the torment I have put her through these past weeks."

"If you truly think so," Audra said doubtfully. "It would be a wonderful thing for Cecily. The greatest of favors. I have no idea how I would ever repay you for such a kindness."

"Do not look so uneasy about it. I would not demand anything unreasonable such as your marrying me, though I still think that would be a very good notion."

"Perhaps it would be, especially when I need to ask you another favor."

He eyed her questioningly.

"I wondered if it is too late . . . That is, could you instruct your estate agent, Mr. Wylie, not to look out for another tenant. I find I am not so eager to . . . to run away as I thought."

Another man might have required more, but Raeburn would never be the sort to need lengthy explanations. He merely held his arms wide, tenderly pronouncing her name.

"Audra."

She stepped into them, burying her face against his shoulder. He held her close, brushing his lips against her hair.

"You must still be patient with me, Raeburn. I have been a spinster for a long time. After watching Mama so often make a fool of herself, I still find the prospect of being in love quite terrifying."

"You think I do not?" he said, pulling her closer. Gazing down at her tenderly, he said, "We shall take all the time that you need. Even after the banns are cried, you will have three weeks to cry off."

He bent to kiss her, when something dropped from his pocket. She was astonished to see that it was a copy of *Ivanhoe*.

"Your sister told me what her dog had done to yours," he said. "I thought I would lend you mine."

Audra seized it eagerly. "I thought I should never know what became of Ivanhoe and his lady at the end of the book."

"If you like," Raeburn said. "I would be only too happy to demonstrate." Yanking her hard against him, his mouth sought hers in a long, lingering kiss.

The hazy thought crossed Audra's mind. In many ways, Raeburn was far superior to anything in her library. As she tightened her arms about him, the book slipped from her grasp entirely unnoticed.